Fic
Ham
C, 2

pb

Hamilton, Virginia
The planet of Junior
Brown

X19736
2.25

DATE DUE	BORROWER'S NAME		
	3950		
DEC 5 '75	Kari		
JAN 20 '78	Berlin		1
MAY 26 '78	Joe Frank		6
MAY 31 1976	Krea		11
APR 1 '84	Tina		22

Fic
Ham
C, 2

Hamilton, Virginia
The planet of Junior Brown
X19736

. . . Seeming to sleep,
slumped down in the collar of his raincoat,
Junior heard Buddy's words in music.
"We are together," Buddy told them,
"because we have to learn
to live for each other."

THE PLANET OF
JUNIOR BROWN
by Virginia Hamilton

"A Planet in this book isn't in the solar system,
it takes no special rockets nor billions of dollars
to reach—you just be willing to share, to follow
directions and to take responsibility. . . .

"There is so much in *The Planet of Junior
Brown*, it could be a poem, or a prayer. That
we as a people seek to be not Junior Browns who
would make music but Tomorrow Billys who
feel 'We are together because we have to learn
to live for each other.' Virginia Hamilton has
taken the children's story into another dimen-
sion right here on earth."

—Nikki Giovanni,
from her review in *Black World*.

Deeply moving, vividly memorable, *The Planet of Junior Brown* will illuminate *your* world. Here is what the critics are saying:

A 1972 NEWBERY MEDAL HONOR BOOK

THE PLANET OF JUNIOR BROWN

VIRGINIA HAMILTON

COLLIER BOOKS

Division of Macmillan Publishing Co., Inc.
New York

Macmillan Publishing Co., Inc.
866 Third Avenue, New York, N.Y. 10022
Collier-Macmillan Canada Ltd.

Library of Congress catalog card number: 71-155264
The Planet of Junior Brown is also published in a
hardcover edition by Macmillan Publishing Co., Inc.

First Collier Books Edition 1974
Printed in the United States of America

For Leigh and Jaime
and the race to come

1

The three of them were hidden in the dark. Enclosed in the forgotten basement room of the school, they were out of our time. One of them had been a janitor in the school for fifteen years. He was Mr. Pool. Once he had been a teacher, an unhappy secret known only by him and the two boys with him.

Long ago, Mr. Pool had constructed a false wall so that the forgotten room appeared to be nothing more than a large broom closet. He had nailed sheet rock to wood studs and had painted it battleship gray. Anyone entering the basement room would see the gray wall with the brooms and mops stacked against it. But only the three of them knew how to move one side of the wall back a foot or two, squeeze into the large room beyond and replace the wall again.

The three of them had entered the room

through the false broom closet many times. And
now, together they watched the feeble light of
the solar system as they had before.

The planets of the solar system were suspended from metal rods which ran along
spherical tracks attached to the ceiling. They
were translucent plastic spheres lighted from
within by tiny Christmas bulbs of red, yellow
and blue. This holiday glow out of the planets
seemed a very distant light. Yet it was the only
light the three of them had and it became a
huge light in the room's musty darkness.

Mr. Pool's head was visible through the
silent swing of the revolving planets. His
head was bald and glistened godlike in the
void. Next to him stood big Buddy Clark.
Buddy had been absent from school and on the
hook for weeks. Now that he and Mr. Pool
had completed their solar system, he thought
he might never go back into that steaming noise
some called the eighth grade. Big Buddy
fiddled with the plastic Halloween pumpkin
which he had painted a hot red to make it
appear more like the sun. Soon his hands were
making motions of magic over all the whirling
planets.

Big Buddy's slender fingers were a match for
the tough set of his jawline. Floating in the
feeble light, his artful hands gave away his
soul in a gentle ritual.

"*I make a world a sto-ray. . . . Do you want to live creation?*" Buddy's fingers seemed to sing in a startling, high song. "*Come listen to my someday . . . how a world made black and brighter rose up righter than its wrong.*"

Mr. Poll's heart swelled with pride. No telling what Buddy would think up next. A boy like him, with a mind like that. Mr. Pool couldn't help saying, "You ought to write that *down*." He knew better than to make Buddy uncomfortable by saying more.

Junior Brown was there with them. He was deeper in the shadow light and dark at the far end of the solar system. Junior sat resting a portion of his huge and rolling fat as best he could in the one folding chair. Bent forward, smiling where Buddy and Mr. Pool couldn't clearly see his expression, he looked like a giant, black Buddha about to topple.

Junior Brown didn't move. He fixed his gaze on the outsized planet of Junior Brown in front of him. Junior loved the planet they had named for him. He should have known Mr. Pool and Buddy could make something he would have to love.

Glazed in beige and black, the planet of Junior Brown was shaped in the soft, round contours of Junior Brown's own face. It was a stupendous mass in a brand new solar system, and it claimed a powerful hold on a green, spinning earth. Earth had become the size of an agate racing along in front of the boundless planet of Junior Brown.

Junior Brown studied his planet, the sun, the earth and the other spheres. Finally he looked across space at the bald head of Mr. Pool and the hands of Buddy Clark cupped in a fixed applause.

"It couldn't happen," Junior said, shaking his head. "That close, the earth wouldn't be nothing by now but a pockmark on the planet of Junior Brown."

Mr. Pool had been watching Junior Brown watch his planet. He hoped the sad, fat boy realized how much work big Buddy had put into the planet of Junior Brown. But maybe the huge fat boy was only a selfish black boy, too heartsick at his own fate to reach out, to touch the fate of another.

No, you do what you can, thought Mr. Pool. You can't expect to save generosity.

"Like yourself," Mr. Pool said, suddenly, speaking to Junior, "astronomers were amazed one morning to discover a new ten-planet solar system right where the nine-planet one had been the morning before. Our earth was a part of the new system; yet it was trapped in the orbit of a fantastic planet known as Junior Brown."

"Then how come the new planet already had

a name when it was only just discovered?" asked Junior. He had spoken as calmly as he could. He still didn't know whether there was a trick somewhere waiting for him.

"Why, it all happened on that morning," said Mr. Pool. "This boy was there at the planetarium early that day looking through the telescope. When he saw what had happened up in space, he commenced to yell for the astronomers.

" 'Hey, looky here!' he kept screaming. Pretty soon, the place was full of sleepy-eyed stargazers. They all knew the boy had no business being in the room where the great telescope was housed.

" 'What's your name, boy?' one of them thought to say.

"The boy, he said, 'Junior Brown! Junior Brown! But looky here in the telescope!'

" 'What's your name again?' one absent-minded professor asked him.

" 'It's Junior Brown! It's Junior Brown! Looky here in the telescope!'

"Well," Mr. Pool said, "finally, they did look through the telescope. One of them said, 'Jesus, Ralph, it really is Junior Brown!'

"What the astronomers saw through their telescope," said Mr. Pool, "changed their lives completely and changed completely the whole order of things. However, the astros were not men to blow their cool. They had a sense of humor.

" 'This might just stop the war for a while,' one of them said. Another said, 'And stop the population explosion.'

" 'And riots,' the boy had said, getting into the swing of it, 'and poverty and going to the Statue of Liberty every field trip day.'

"After that," said Mr. Pool, "Junior Brown was always welcome at the planetarium. The astronomers never caught what his name was and never knew how they happened to call the amazing new planet, Junior Brown. But they were glad to have a name for it right off like that. Now, they wouldn't have to name it My Old Lady, which had been the suggestion of one graduate assistant."

"Oh, sure, man," Buddy Clark said, taking up the story from Mr. Pool. Buddy's voice was a soft, high purr. "Those astronomers measured and experimented and even ate their meals looking through that telescope. They had to admit that the ten-planet solar system after about fifty thousand years was stable and up there to stay for the rest of time."

In the feeble light of the miniature solar system, Big Buddy's hands flipped over, palms down. His hands crossed and slowly uncrossed, while in the room the planets slowed into gliding, peaceful revolutions.

There were three speeds to Mr. Pool's and Buddy Clark's solar system, the same as there were to any decent record player. It was Mr. Pool who had changed the pace of the planets while Junior watched Buddy's hands. But for Junior the slowing down of the planets had seemed like magic.

"Now," Buddy said, "just figure how those astronomers felt when it hit 'em that little earth wasn't a bit bothered by what had to be a hot-stuff gravity pull from the planet of Junior Brown. Shoot, man, they tore out their hair. Eyeballs were spinning!" Buddy Clark laughed. To Junior, the laughter spilled out of Buddy's mouth in musical triads.

"Remember." Mr. Pool spoke again. "Earth didn't circle the great planet like a satellite. It revolved around the sun in orbit with and in front of the planet of Junior Brown."

In shadow and light, Junior Brown tried to keep calm. Mr. Pool and Buddy could do anything, could make anything they wanted to make. It seemed to Junior that he couldn't do anything anymore, not even the one thing he wanted most to do. Behind his eyes, the sound of Miss Lynora Peebs' grand piano swelled in a perfect crescendo as he played it.

The music of his mind faded as Junior concentrated on what Mr. Pool had just told him.

It's some kind of math problem, he thought.

He studied the orbiting earth and the planet of
Junior Brown. Then he watched Mr. Pool.
Junior's face was placid when at last he said,
"There's no way to balance the earth against
the pull of a planet the size of Junior Brown."

"Indeed," Mr. Pool said. "And when the
astros calculated the planet's weight, they
found it solid beyond all wishing otherwise.

"However," Mr. Pool added, "everything
worked out just fine when a band of some thirty
asteroids was discovered in the same orbit and
at exactly the same distance from the planet of
Junior Brown as was its leader, earth."

"My stars," said Buddy Clark, "I think I spy
me an equation."

Junior Brown brushed his hand over his
eyes. He should have known Buddy would
have to pull some trick—just because he knew
some science. Buddy couldn't play the piano,
though, the way Junior could. He couldn't
paint people, either.

"I don't see no thirty asteroids following the
planet of Junior Brown," Junior said.

There was silence in the room before Buddy
thought to say, "You don't see any moon going
around the earth, either, man."

"I meant to ask you about that, too," Junior
said. "And the sun you made won't be near
big enough, either."

"Listen at this clown," Buddy said to Mr.

Pool. His magical hands fell away into the darkness. "We had enough trouble adding an extra planet, didn't we, Mr. Pool?" And then: "You ever try to figure out the problems to adding a tenth planet to a nine-planet solar system?" he said to Junior. "Well, then, you should next think about trying to figure a band of asteroids to boot."

"If and when you going to build something, built it right," Junior told him.

"He always got to spoil something," Buddy said to Mr. Pool. "How you ever going to change a clown who don't have to want for nothing . . ."

"Didn't spoil nothing," Junior cut in on him. "I just didn't see no asteroids and you all started in talking about some asteriods."

"He want gold-plated asteroids and a fifty-foot sun made from silver," muttered Buddy. "I had hard enough time stealing a motor to run this whole thing."

Mr. Pool's head spun to one side. "You stole it? You didn't steal it, Buddy!"

"Naw!" Buddy said, clenching his hands in the feeble light. "I didn't steal it offen no-body!"

"Then why you say you stole it when you know you never did?" Junior said. He smirked at catching Buddy in a lie.

"Because, clown, it's easier to say I stole it

than to tell how much of a steal it was picking it up in the street."

"Shuh," Junior said. "Motor lying there, jumping around on the corner. Say, 'Here I am, Buddy, come on, put me in your solar system.'" Junior laughed, his body rolling and shaking.

"Okay," Buddy said, "I got me a mechanism off of one cat in the gas station on Amsterdam and I got me another piece from a body shop on Canal. Pretty soon, I got all the parts and I put me together a motor, and that's the truth."

"You could of told us that in the first place," Junior said, "making out how you so tough, stealing a motor out of some store."

"I never did say I stole it out of no store!" Buddy exploded.

"Boys!" Mr. Pool said sharply. "Cut it out now. Let's get back to the solar system." He waited a moment for them to quiet down. Then he began again. "We all agree that the asteroids should be there following the planet of Junior Brown. Since they aren't, because Buddy and I didn't build them, we'll have to pretend they are there."

"He's just always got to be so right," Buddy couldn't help saying about Junior.

Junior Brown stayed quiet. He tried again to appreciate the fun they'd been having but he had already separated himself from it. He was outside of it, for fear it would turn on him.

"There's a band of asteroids right behind the planet of Junior Brown," Junior said. "I see a whole bunch of thirty of them."

"That's right," said Mr. Pool. "The asteroids and earth make two equilateral triangles with the planet of Junior Brown and the sun."

Then Buddy said, "Any three bodies in space forming an equilateral triangle will revolve in a circular orbit around one of the three . . ."

"I know it," Junior said softly. He wished he could just go home to his room. But he continued. "One triangle is Junior Brown, the asteroids and the sun. And the other is Junior Brown, the earth and the sun. It comes from the Lagrange proof that every planet will have in its orbit two points of gravitational equilibrium where matter could settle . . ."

"Good for you," Mr. Pool told Junior. "I hope you can see that each point would be the third corner of an equilateral triangle formed by drawing lines between it and the planet and the sun."

Junior looked from Mr. Pool to Buddy, then down to the spheres of the solar system. He was feeling pretty good inside, for Mr. Pool and Buddy had gone to a lot of trouble to take his mind off things. Junior always did like to play games. Only this planet of Junior Brown was almost more attention and kindness than he could stand. Rocking gently back and forth, he cupped both hands over his eyes.

Understanding Junior's shyness, Mr. Pool thought to look away. He turned toward Buddy Clark, who stood bathing his hands in the feeble light. Buddy seemed not to know what to do next to show his regard for the huge and talented, often helpless fat boy.

Mr. Pool smiled at the wonder of Buddy Clark, for seldom had Mr. Pool come across a street boy like him. He had found Buddy a year ago in the straggly, rough-house pit of the seventh grade. Hidden until the school was empty and looking like any half-wild alley cat, Buddy had crept from his hiding place and had picked the lock of the nearest classroom. Once inside, Buddy had opened a book he had with him and had filled the chalkboard with math problems beyond his comprehension.

So it had seemed, thought Mr. Pool.

Watching from the shadows of a year ago, he had discovered that Buddy could get through two or three problems difficult even for a college student. Weeks later Mr. Pool had thought of taking over a forgotten basement room and making it into a hidden place from where he might help and teach the boy.

But a year ago, skittish and suspicious of any adult, Buddy Clark had bolted. He hadn't sneaked back into the classroom at night for a month. The next time Mr. Pool saw him, Buddy had Junior Brown with him.

Junior Brown. A year ago Mr. Pool had seen Junior around. He'd heard Junior playing the piano in the music room but he hadn't gone near him.

With his talent, Junior should have been given all the care he needed. But so fat, so awful to look at. The school, like Mr. Pool, had left him alone.

From the very first he had been careful of the two boys. Last year, letting them know he was there in the shadows, he had kept his distance and was as cautious as any teacher ought to be.

Mathematics cushioned by astronomy had long ago been Mr. Pool's waking thought. Surely he had been successful in his classroom teaching. Tough, black children of city streets could lay bare their minds in his loud and open classes.

But I lost heart, thought Mr. Pool. I could no longer teach in so rigid a regime. Maybe I was wrong. Things change—has any of it really changed?

Only now, through his work with Buddy Clark and the example of Buddy's devotion to Junior Brown, did Mr. Pool slowly begin to believe in himself again. He could no longer remember when he arrived at the curious notion that the two-legged beings on earth were only disguised as men. Working with Buddy, he sensed a whole new being lying in wait within the boy.

Perhaps the human race is yet to come, thought Mr. Pool. We must make life ready.

Buddy Clark moved through the darkness of the hidden room with its solar system until he was standing beside Junior Brown. Gently he feinted a couple of left jabs to Junior's head and succeeded in easing the fat boy out of himself.

"Shuh, man," Junior said, half in anger. Swinging one of his enormous arms, he knocked Buddy away into darkness.

Buddy laughed, surprised, as he always did when reminded of the sheer strength of Junior Brown. Above them in the school, buzzers sounded, followed by muffled scuffling, like hundreds of rats trapped in an attic.

"Two-fifteen," Buddy said. "We still got us some time." He looked down at the mighty planet of Junior Brown. "Let them crack those books."

Junior Brown shifted his bulk in the folding chair. "I thought I'd maybe leave early," he said. He did not look at Buddy.

Buddy was silent a moment. Lately, Junior would try to get away by himself. Buddy never could figure out if Junior was trying to get rid of him.

"You leave early," Buddy said, "and you going to have to go down to the river and wait longer than you would ordinary, since it's Friday, anyway."

Immediately, Buddy knew he shouldn't have mentioned Friday. He could have kicked himself when he saw Junior trying to hide his 262-pound body within the flab of his arms.

"Listen, man," Buddy said to Junior, "Mr. Pool and me, we haven't even finished our entertainment. We got us a whole show ready —how much you know about our universe?"

Junior had to shake his head, for what he knew about the universe had come from his friendship with Buddy Clark. He never felt close to it the way he felt close to music. The feel of space between quarter notes or the arrangement of space in an arpeggio played properly made Junior completely happy. But the rhythms of the universe and the vastness of its space brought him only loneliness.

"Mr. Pool here knows all about the universe," Buddy said. "Nothing he don't know, so you can set yourself easy, Junior, we going to give you a circus ride."

Mr. Pool waited in the weak glow of the planets to see if Buddy could reassure the fat boy for one more time.

What would happen, he wondered, if Buddy got tired of it and let Junior leave early? Would Junior hurry off? Or would he stay, afraid to move without big Buddy to shadow him?

Mr. Pool's hands came into the light, touching spheres as they moved, and testing the rods from which they were suspended.

"The universe," he said, "has to be the same everywhere, in all directions. Our solar system in the Milky Way is not unusual or different. Our own planet of Junior Brown in the solar system is quite ordinary."

Junior Brown knew his planet was huge in the solar system but only a speck in the Milky Way.

"Heavenly science demonstrates that nature is the same everywhere," Mr. Pool said. "The universe acts the same everywhere. This being so, the Milky Way, the solar system and the planet of Junior Brown hold no unusual position."

"Space and time," Buddy Clark said. He let the feeble light slip through his fingers. "Energy, matter, gravitation and light."

"Not space," said Mr. Pool, "nor light nor any of the others can be measured alone, but only in relation to one or more of the others."

Alone.

Across the span of planets, Junior Brown thought, Who am I? What can I know? It's Friday. Outside me, it might be Monday. Or nothing. Or something terrible.

"Earth creatures will not survive forever," droned Mr. Pool. "Our solar system, our Milky Way, will not survive. Travel to other galaxies will remain impossible . . ." He sighed. ". . . for movement in space seems not to exceed the speed of light. Traveling at the speed of light, it would take a being two million years to reach Andromeda, our neighboring galaxy. . . ."

Soon buzzers again sounded above the three of them. ". . . When the youngest stars of our Milky Way die as all things will die," said Mr. Pool, "life for beings will end."

Junior Brown got up slowly from his chair, his unbelievable girth of flesh and fat spreading out from his powerful frame.

If all things were bound to die, what was the point of being born? Junior thought.

"*A'm lookin' forty mile,*" he sang softly to himself, "*Believe a'm fixin' ta die . . .*" He moved away from the light of the solar system into the void.

"Wait a minute, man," Buddy told him.

"I got to hurry, I got me someplace to go," Junior said.

"I know all about someplace you got to go," said Buddy. "It's Friday, man."

Buddy scrambled through the dark after Junior. When they both were within the false broom closet, they began groping around on the dark floor. After a moment Junior found his Fake Book. In no way false, the Fake Book was a thick volume of jazz and rock tunes arranged and copied professionally and in keys suitable for the average singer. The book had cost Junior's mother fifty dollars. Junior always carried the book although he never used the arrangements. But hidden inside were his music lessons and his own classical compositions.

Next Junior found a pile of torn and battered textbooks. He grabbed a couple of books and placed them safely with his Fake Book under his arm. Buddy took a couple of books also. Then, facing the door, the two of them stood side by side waiting tensely for Mr. Pool to release them.

In the hidden room, Mr. Pool turned off the lights of the solar system by shutting off the system's power source. In the total darkness, he stalked the planets until he found the big one called Junior Brown. The planet hung at a height the level of his chest. Mr. Pool found it with his hands on his first attempt.

He had to smile. Superstitious, he couldn't help suspecting that the planet of Junior Brown vanished as though it never existed once its light was turned off.

But the planet of Junior Brown was safe in the room. That, to Mr. Pool, was a great comfort.

In a moment Mr. Pool stood in the broom closet. Opening the door slightly, he listened awhile to the tramping feet, the noise of children. Then he called softly to Junior and Buddy that they could leave.

"I don't need to remind you . . ." he said.

"No," said Buddy.

"I will anyway," said Mr. Pool. "One of these days we're going to get caught."

"Right on," Buddy said.

"Further on," Junior said.

"And they will get rid of me, like maybe they've been itching to do for years," Mr. Pool said.

"We're sorry about that," Buddy said, his voice rougher now.

"You are not to worry," Mr. Pool said. "They'll fire me and we'll get together with the solar system somewheres else."

Buddy and Junior slipped quickly through the door. They tiptoed down the long hall which turned twice, until they had reached the outer door.

Buddy Clark took a bunch of keys from his pocket and unlocked the triple police lock. Outside, a line of students streamed down the steps at the front of the school. When the stream was large enough to become raucous, Buddy rushed up the basement steps with Junior close behind him. In the mass of students the boys separated. Alone, neither of them registered on the mind in any special way. For one more time they had worked their escape.

Buddy hummed to himself as he always did at the moment he knew that he and Junior were going to make it. Two blocks beyond the school he saw Junior, whom he had allowed to pass him, and caught up with him.

Junior didn't look around when Buddy came up beside him.

"You got anything particular in your mind?" Buddy asked him.

"Just me going to the river," Junior told him. He didn't feel like talking to Buddy anymore, or anyone. The effort of talking and walking at the same time took his breath.

"I'll just go with you," Buddy said, "make sure you don't slip and fall in that messy water."

"Not going to fall. Even if I did, I can swim enough," Junior told him.

"Shoot," Buddy said. "You is big as a boulder and you would sink as fast as a boulder."

"Shuh," Junior said. He refused to speak to Buddy for the rest of the way.

2

Junior loved the low sky and the Hudson River surrounded by zero winter. The river was smooth. Breaking into it was a light of yellow mist out of a sky the color of sulfur and filled with fumes from chemicals. The sky above the river was vibrant with cold poison, the kind of sky Junior felt he knew best. Cold winter was the one season he could be outdoors and feel comfortable seeing the day. In this late November he wore only a yellow Dacron shirt and brown denim trousers.

The river looked clean. The putrid light out of the sky made New Jersey on the far bank seem a fantasy Christmas land atop the Palisades. These past weeks Junior had needed Jersey to seem as unreal as possible. He had needed to wipe it away with a flick of his hand over his vision, if only he could.

"*A'm a low-life clown, with muh head on upside dow-ow-wown,*" he sang.

He and Buddy had climbed the iron fence on the bank of the river and now braced themselves against boulders at the water's edge. They filled their pockets with rocks. Here there were rats living on the river's filth. Not even freezing winter could rid the shore of its awful smell.

"I can't stand it, whew!" Buddy said.

"Shuh," Junior told him. He wished Buddy would just disappear.

"But I'm cold. I already froze myself getting here," Buddy said, "and you going to freeze yourself too." Buddy wore his windbreaker; even so the weather coming off the water went right through it.

"Whyn't you go on home then?" Junior said. "Nobody ask you to freeze your diaper out here."

They settled down uncomfortably on icy rocks. Junior put his Fake Book and torn textbooks carefully down beside him. He was feeling mean toward Buddy and impatient with the slow passage of time. He could tell by the dull yellow light closing in on them that the time was about three-thirty. He still had a whole hour to get down to 79th Street and Broadway.

They saw a rat move boldly. It was big and hungry, with hair almost black. Swiftly Buddy aimed and threw a stone all in one sure motion. The stone grazed the rat.

"He ain't going to move. He thinking about fightin' back," Junior said.

Buddy hurled three stones in succession; one whucked sickeningly against the rat's side. The rat's hindquarters quivered; then it moved off under rocks.

Once at 79th and Broadway, Junior would have to go one block down to 78th Street and one block east to Amsterdam Avenue. Behind his eyes, those streets were blown clean by cold wind. Apartment-house lobbies on 78th would be free of the usual scarred tables in anticipation of holiday decoration.

He could take a subway at 96th and Broadway and be down at 79th Street in less than fifteen minutes. Even though he was slow, he knew he could make that block from 79th to 78th Street and the one block over to Amsterdam in five, seven minutes.

Be there thirty minutes early, Junior thought. I don't know what I'll do if she won't let me play. I should of told Mama about it. Shuh, Mama wouldn't of believed me—how you going to tell her something like what's been happening? She'd think I was just trying to get out of the lessons.

Buddy sat hunched over, freezing. He imagined his face turning ashen with cold. His toes were numb and his nose had started running. The moisture in his nostrils crystallized, forcing him to breathe through his mouth. Buddy made himself sit silently so he could watch Junior with the least amount of physical pain to himself.

All sorts of moods played over Junior's face and all of them upset Buddy. Buddy could tell that Junior was still carrying on to himself. There had been a time when all of Junior's thoughts had been open to Buddy.

"We might take us a bus," Buddy said, in a bursting loud rush right in Junior's ear. "We early for your lesson."

"You can't come in with me!" Junior was shouting. "You know you can't so why you keep on following me?"

"One of these times I'm going to leave you by yourself and see how you like it," Buddy told him.

"Like it fine," Junior said. "Maybe then I can have some peace in my brains."

They both fell silent. There were two rats at the water line off to their left but neither of them bothered to stone them. Buddy was ashamed at feeling hurt that Junior didn't want him around. He knew he was getting on Junior's nerves. Lately he had stuck with Junior from the time Junior came out of his apartment house in the morning to the time he went back in at night. Buddy let Junior go into his house alone because Junior's mother didn't want her fat son to associate with him. And Buddy let Junior go alone from 78th Street and on into Miss Peebs' house on Amsterdam to take his piano lesson each and every Friday.

Buddy Clark had known Junior's mother long enough and well enough to understand that she wasn't the cause of the change in Junior. Junior Brown's mother was as out of her head anxious as all the other women in the neighborhood whose husbands had gone away. Only, Junior's father had a good job over in Jersey. But just like the other women, Junior's mother had all the time she needed to get her insides confused and to make the life of her favorite child over to suit herself. In Junella Brown's case, it was her only child.

Maybe she is sickly, the way she likes to say, thought Buddy. She still uses that asthma of hers to keep Junior as close to home as she can.

He got himself a piano in his very own room, Buddy went on to himself. He got books and a raincoat. He even gets rolls of canvas and paints for to draw with. And still he says he'd just as soon have nothing if he could have his daddy come home every night and be there every morning. He lucky he got a "daddy" at all, but he don't know *nothing*.

Mrs. Junella Brown bothered Junior into going out to restaurants and to uplifting plays.

Buddy shot a quick glance to the center of the river. A few chunks of ice floated easily along. They seemed rounded, perhaps melting. Buddy hunched his shoulders and clenched his frozen fists, hoping for a thaw.

"I saw you and your maw going out last night," he said. Upriver there was more ice.

"Trying to be some kind of detective," Junior told him. "Join up with the Force and they'll get you a badge with Captain Oink written over it."

"I happened to be coming down the street," Buddy said. "When I see you all coming out, I ducked myself into the building across the way."

"Duck yourself, nothing," Junior said. "You standing there hiding and waiting."

Buddy decided he'd better get on with it. He had been waiting across the street from Junior's house. He didn't know why, or what he hoped to see. His nights were always too long. He could go to what he called home, but he only went there to leave something or to pick something up. Usually he ended up somewhere near the building where Junior lived.

His story was that there in the city his mama was actually his aunt. Buddy's real mama was still in East Texas with the rest of

the kids. She was trying to save to get the rest
of the kids and herself up here. Buddy kept
on telling her to stay where she was. There
wasn't nothing up here but trash and terror,
he wrote her. And his aunt, who was his
mother's sister, kept hounding him to quit
school. Grow up, she told him. Go work in
the garment district and do something for your
helpless mother.

Buddy smiled. In his head, he had this long
conversation with this person who was his
aunt, all about how he loved school and how
he was going to go on to college.

Maybe I will go to college, he thought.
Maybe some billionaire will give me ten dollars a minute and a gold pot to keep it in too.

This was his story known to Junior and to
Mr. Pool. The truth was, Buddy was by himself.

"You and your maw go to some kind of
Broadway play last night?" Buddy said.

Junior took his time about answering. He
finally said, "We went us to Weight Watchers.
I bet you haven't ever heard of the Weight
Watchers."

"I heard," Buddy said, evenly, although the
idea surprised him. "What did they make you
do?"

"Make me do nothing," Junior told him.

"They stared at me a lot and I didn't like that one bit."

"What kind of else did they do?" Buddy asked him.

"They talked a lot about celery and raw mushrooms."

"Gawd," Buddy said.

"They seem to think pretty highly of broiled fish."

"Nobody eat that stuff," Buddy said.

"Then one lady, she say maybe how I abuse my body because I didn't much care for my black skin." Junior laughed softly to himself, his fat shaking and rolling under his shirt. "Ole white lady," he added. "She had on this red coat and this red fur hat. She had real orange hair and she was wearing a shiny brown dress. She wasn't bad, but she was pretty plump herself."

"Might be some truth in what she saying," Buddy said. "I mean, eating so much because you so black."

"Shuh," Junior said. "You're black but you don't eat the way I do. I seen some white folks just as fat as me. And anyway, black is beautiful." He had to laugh.

"Did they put you on some diet?" Buddy said.

"Say Mama have to cook me a little bitty this without no oil," Junior told him, "and a little bitty that without no butter or no flour or no nothing."

"She'll do it, too," Buddy said.

"Hush off my mother," Junior said. "She sickly."

Sickly like a night tripper, like a fox. Buddy didn't say what he had been thinking. Right then he decided it wasn't Junior's mother or the Weight Watchers or the black of Junior's skin that was causing him to be so nervous and full of secrets. There was only one change in Junior's life and that was Miss Peebs.

Buddy had a sudden memory of a nicer time. Junior had taken piano lessons from the age of five. He had known Miss Peebs for six months. Over the summer, somebody Miss Peebs knew managed to get Junior on the stage in a concert at Central Park. Buddy had been thrilled to see his friend up there at the piano in the bandshell, with all the people from all over stopping their strolls to sit and listen. It was the most exciting thing Buddy had ever seen. Big, fat and black Junior Brown playing classical music—even Buddy had to admit the music sounded fine—and then getting all that applause when he was finished. And then Junior coming down off that stage to sit right next to Buddy. That had been the best part of all. Buddy recalled he had met that Miss Peebs but she had been just some lady. She hadn't seemed important and he didn't remember much about her. But now Junior had something worrying him, something he couldn't tell Buddy.

Junior sat there by the water worrying about Buddy asking him so many questions. He was afraid he might talk too much. He wanted to talk now. If he only could talk, but how could he say anything?

Junior got up, moving in a crouch. Holding onto boulders when he could, he made his way up the rocks toward the iron fence.

"You leaving now?" Buddy called after him. The sky had changed, shading into gray before it would turn into night. Buddy followed Junior, holding back his strength and easy movement to give the fat boy room.

He had all kinds of ideas about Junior and that Miss Peebs, whom he'd only once seen. He was a champ. He knew everything the street could teach him.

Buddy stared after the grunting form of Junior Brown. No matter how completely Junior had changed into someone nervous and frustrated, he was still the shyest, most innocent boy Buddy had ever known.

"*Junior, you're trying to give up on one more thing.*" Junior's mother reached into Junior's mind and tried to take it over. Her sudden presence caused Junior to slip on the rocks and fall to his knees.

Junior groaned and sat down, rubbing his shinbone.

"*Do you want me to believe you haven't the courage to face your talent?*"

"*Mama, why you always have to bust in on me?*" Junior's head throbbed as he realized the mama of his mind believed he was afraid to take his lesson.

Buddy scrambled over the rocks and tried to get Junior to his feet. "Are you hurt?" he said. "Looky, you gone and tore your pants at the knee." Buddy tried to lift Junior under the arms. Big and strong, he still couldn't budge Junior. "Come on, get up," Buddy said. "We can take us a bus right on Riverside Drive and you won't have to walk so far."

"*Don't you dare to get on a bus!*" Junior's mother let loose her fear. "*You'll never get there if you get on a bus!*"

Junior's shoulders were wrenched once in a sob and then were still. He bowed his head, trying to think. The voice bursting in on him at any time had weakened his nerve. He was on the verge of blurting something about Miss Peebs, so he started talking as fast as he could.

Buddy sat down in front of Junior, stunned by Junior's stream of words.

"Seven-thirty," Junior said. "We were all finished with the Weight Watchers. I promised Mama I would come back again. I had to do that. They were all waiting for me to say how

I would lose ten pounds by next week and
come back to lose some more. You know how
I can't stop eating once I get started. I just
can't keep from it. I get out of bed and I don't
even know it. I'm at the refrigerator and I
don't even realize. I eat it all up, everything.
I cook the eggs, bacon—and it's like I'm thinking about something miles away and I don't
know. I never remember I shouldn't be eating
until it's too late.

"We left the Weight Watchers and Mama
kept on saying how nice everybody had been.
She still think they gonna lynch you if you go
downtown too far."

"She halfway right, too," Buddy couldn't
help saying.

"Anyway," Junior said, "she got started on
how we ought to get out of our black world
more. With Daddy gone all week, we are getting to be like hermits, was what she told me.
I didn't say nothing because I was hungry and
I just wanted us to get on home. And then
Mama took this envelope out of her pocket-
book. She say to me, 'Junior, look here what I
have for us. We are going out tonight.' Right
then I began to sweat because in the envelope
she had two tickets for a concert at the big
Lincoln Center for the Performing Arts. Mama
say to me, 'Junior, it is a modern dance concert
we are going to see.'

"And I say to her, 'Mama, please, just let me go on home. I got to get me some rest. Please, these Weight Watchers have got me all upset.'

"Mama, she say, 'Junior, you are not going to hide out in your room. You have nothing to be ashamed of. A little overgrown you may well be but, Junior, you are *talented* and you will not hide!'

"I was wearing my gray suit and my raincoat. Mama, she had on a black dress and that black coat she has with the fur at the collar. She even had her medicine with her. We both looked all right but once we were practically there," said Junior, "I got to thinking that everybody would stare at us. By the time we were in the lobby, it looked to me like everybody was shrinking away from me. You know, like they were trying to keep from looking at my fat. And Mama, she looked like she wasn't sure of what she was doing. Even she started to shrink away.

"And then I had a hard time fitting into my seat," Junior said. "I started wheezing, the way Mama does when she's sick. It took all I had just to sit still in my suit and that raincoat, with Mama whispering at me to control my breath.

"The curtain went up and we saw this program of dance groups. Or maybe it was just one group—how can you tell when they melt away and come back again? All I could see was a lot of thin people jumping and falling. I thought I couldn't breathe and there was this white lady next to me all full of awful-sweet powder. By the end of the show, I was soaking wet and I got to shaking like some wino."

The whole time Junior talked, Buddy sat before him. His eyes never left Junior's face. One moment, Buddy wrung his hands and the next, he stuffed them deep in his pockets. All his own tough coolness slipped away as he came to understand the awful ugliness Junior felt about himself. Sitting there listening and watching, Buddy could be, for a few seconds at a time, Junior Brown wanting to hide himself from the whole world.

Junior managed to get to his feet. Without a word he started again for the iron fence.

"Man?" Buddy said.

For one more time, Junior had managed to keep from talking about Miss Peebs' piano.

Buddy stood up with the light out of the sky behind him. He closed his eyes, then opened them. He held his body tight together with his shoulders hunched close to his ears.

Buddy had helped all kinds of people. In the streets he had found all sorts of people who were hurt bad. But every time he tried to help Junior, Junior thought he was feeling sorry for him. Giving a hand to somebody hurt wasn't something you did out of pity. Buddy could help somebody without thinking about it and without feeling anything. With Junior he thought he knew how hard it was to even walk when you were so big and fat.

It's just that Junior looks at you like you've already beat him up once, Buddy thought. And to have the kind of mother he's got—I'd take the street any day—not even to speak about what kind of hold that Miss Peebs must have on him.

Buddy allowed himself to catch up with Junior at the broad walkway high above the river, near the playground at 97th Street. At Junior's side once more, Buddy let himself ease into Junior's mood. Soon they were again together in some unspoken regard.

There were many cars on the street called Riverside Drive. There were lots of people, folks who lived in the tall, orderly apartment buildings lining the street. Buddy looked up at the buildings with something close to awe. He could imagine the good life of those folks living in the buildings, he just couldn't see himself ever living there or having such a life.

No way, he thought. He felt suddenly tired. His body ached from the cold.

In this neighborhood Junior and Buddy walked closer to one another, with their

shoulders sometimes touching. They were both
tall. They looked older than their years and
their sudden, loud energy often scared people.
Buddy was as muscled and well proportioned
as a college freshman just out of high school
playing fields. Junior was huge and oddly
graceful, like a man who has lived comforta-
bly with his fat for a long time. His face with
its smooth black skin was so round, his eyes
appeared to be swollen closed into slits. He
had no eyebrows to speak of, just two lines of
movement above his eyes which drooped toward his temples in a permanent expression of
sadness.

Junior was soaked through with sweat in two
oblong circles under his arms. That was the
reason Buddy paused at the bus stop as though
it had been decided they would take a bus.
Not saying a word, Junior went on. If he were
to get on a bus this time of day, he could
usually find two empty seats together. He could
sit down. Hiding himself there in the rear of
the bus, he could look like anybody else of
ordinary size. He could stay on the bus for as
long as he wanted, usually to the end of the
downtown line.

At the bus stop on 97th Street, Junior started
across to the opposite corner. The light had
turned green by the time Buddy saw him.
Buddy had to cross against the traffic; he put

out his hands menacingly to the cars. Tires screeched. One driver came too close and yelled something. Buddy didn't bother to worry about what someone tried to say.

Probably think I'm some alcoholic. Buddy grinned at the cars and spun around once on his heels before leaping onto the curb on the other side of the Drive. He saw the Riverside bus coming down the winding hill above 99th Street. He watched it a moment and then turned away toward Broadway.

The two of them reached Broadway and Junior's face was burning hot under the skin. His body tingled from the effort of keeping it moving. Itching, the very top of his head felt as though it had detached itself from the rest. Junior was lightheaded. The sensation that his scalp was floating had been with him for days.

Junior loved Broadway. He knew he belonged to it the way the fixtures of newsstands and traffic lights belonged to it. The wide avenue had its lanes of uptown and downtown traffic divided by concrete islands. The islands had green benches, grass and bushes. A few trees struggled to grow in an atmosphere choked with automobile exhaust fumes. Junior found all of it beautiful—the stunted trees, the winter-brown plants and the old men and women. Out of the cheap retirement rooms of the side streets, the lonely old people rested awhile, like lost bundles on the cold, sunny benches. In summer the old folks were joined by young drug trippers. And nodding together in the light, they would all cover the island benches from noon to dusk.

Odors from the bakery and the fresh-fish store wafted on the cold air as Junior and Buddy walked toward the subway. Junior felt heat with a scent of raw meat coming from the supermarket as the entrance door opened and closed for customers.

And the people. Junior loved the people walking on Broadway. He longed to have a full look at the different faces he saw passing him. Not aware of what he was doing, Junior moved away from Buddy into the flow of people coming toward him. He lifted his hand as if to touch a profile here and a full face there. Without looking at him the people walking on Broadway sidestepped Junior. Knowing they might run into someone like him at any moment, they left him standing in the middle of the sidewalk with his hand raised.

"Don't *do* that!" Buddy whispered at him, taking his arm. "I told you before, you can't do that, people don't like that."

The two of them moved together through the crowd. Junior had not said a word. Buddy had to keep him moving, for Junior was still seeing and longing for the faces. Into the separate places of his mind he sorted features of black Haitians and Puerto Ricans from black Americans. Later, in his room, he would draw them all. The many Jews he saw Junior kept apart from all other groups. Jews were a contradiction in his mind and out of it. By design, they kept themselves separate; they would have been shocked to find themselves trapped inside Junior's head.

Junior's mind gave every Jew he saw a powerful place on Broadway. Here they owned businesses or they were teachers, doctors, lawyers. They allowed the blacks to seize the apartment houses on the side streets while they held onto their enormous buildings on the avenues.

The overwhelming noise of Broadway throbbed in Junior's head. He had been walking as if in a trance, guided toward the subway by Buddy Clark.

Something stirred inside Junior. He remembered. In the basement room of the school just today Buddy had asked Mr. Pool something— *"Is one folk measured only in relation to some other folk"*—that was it. But Junior couldn't remember what Mr. Pool had answered.

The top of Junior's head itched with a new intensity. It seemed to lift away from his skull. At the pay booth in the subway he fumbled for change in his pockets with fingers that could not grasp.

"Keep your hands at your sides before you

get into trouble," Buddy told Junior. "I've got the right money for both of us."

"What am I going to do?" Junior said. "I won't never get through the turnstile."

"Man, what's the matter with you?" Buddy said. "Do like you always do. I tell the lady at the booth. We put the money in right where she can see. I go through and hold open the exit door for you and then I go out and go through the turnstile again."

"She won't let us," Junior said.

The lady in the booth watched them closely but she let them pass through the way Buddy had planned.

"You worry about everything but what you need to worry about," Buddy said to Junior. "I'm telling you, you ought to see yourself on Broadway, just standing there staring at people going by and then walking like you asleep. Like some nut—that's what you ought to be worrying about."

I maybe could tell about it to Daddy, Junior thought, but he is there working in Jersey and staying the nights, too. If and when he gets home on a Saturday, I've been to the lesson and I can't talk about it.

Buddy steered Junior along the platform to where they could catch a local train which would make more frequent stops.

I never do feel like talking about it until

around Wednesday. I get to thinking about Friday and how something might've happened and how I won't stand it if it has, even when I know there's nothing I can do.

They heard the train coming before they saw it. It pulled into the station. There were many people getting out. Buddy Clark pushed his way into the car. Junior waited until all the people were out of his way. The door was about to close again. Still Junior didn't move. Buddy rushed to the door to hold it open.

"Man!" he said. He jerked Junior forward so that Junior fell inside the train in a rush of his own weight.

"I've got to make sure." Junior's mind spoke to him. "I've got to see it and play on the keys this time, just for a little while."

3

an I come in?" Junior called through the door. He was breathless and aching to rest. He banged on the door for all he was worth. "Can I please come in and sit myself down?"

For longer than a minute there was silence on the other side of the door. Junior sensed that Miss Peebs was there waiting, deciding whether she would let him enter for one more time. Finally there was movement and the sound of locks being released. First Miss Peebs unlocked the two chain locks. Next she opened the spring bolt lock. And last she unlocked the police lock and removed the heavy iron bar from its mechanism.

When Lynora Peebs opened the door for Junior Brown, she was dressed in red slacks under a finger-length dressing gown similar to a kimono. She looked younger than her fifty-six years, as though time had forgotten about her at the age of thirty-nine. Her skin was light brown with a yellowish tint glowing through a girlish smoothness. Her eyes were black and feverish in their narrow oval shapes. There was no bridge to her nose and her graying hair had been straightened with a hot comb and pulled back in a flip ponytail. Lynora Peebs' feet were shoeless and heavily powdered. She had told Junior once that she powdered her feet so she could follow her footprints and know when anyone crossed her path. Junior had laughed when she told him that but Lynora Peebs had not even smiled.

"Can I come in?" Junior said again.

"Be quiet," Miss Peebs told him. "Junior Brown, I don't know how you are going to take your lesson today."

"Yes, ma'am," Junior said. "Why is that?" He eased his bulk around her and into the foyer.

"As you may well remember, I had to destroy the piano," Miss Pebbs said.

"I can take the lesson on a chair, using my fingers." How many weeks had Junior been telling her that? He had spoken in a flat tone, as though reciting a boring line of poetry. "I can prop my music up and beat the lesson out on a chair."

"It's so hard for me to concentrate on harmony," Miss Peebs said softly.

"Yes, ma'am," Junior told her. "Don't you worry about that." His voice was as gentle as he felt toward her. He longed to be able to talk openly with Miss Peebs the way he used to. There had been a time when she would sit him down and tell him stories of her family. He in turn had told her about his most private dreams.

Their conversation every Friday had become no more than a ceremony. Miss Peebs had for weeks greeted him with the news that she had destroyed her piano. The first time she had told Junior that, she had refused to let him into her apartment. Finally Junior had thought of telling her he could beat out his lesson on a chair. With that, Miss Peebs had allowed him to come inside. But she would never go into her living room while he was there, nor let him practice on her grand piano. Junior had not attempted to enter the living room out of respect for Miss Peebs' wishes. But every day he found himself worrying about her piano. Each Friday, the urge to play the piano grew stronger.

Now that Junior was in the apartment, his fear for the piano settled back into the steady pounding of his heart. Almost patiently, he waited for the ceremony to continue, for Miss Peebs to make tea, which they would sip while he beat out his lesson.

"Be quiet!" Lynora said suddenly. Junior had not moved from where he leaned against the wall. He turned his head slowly and found

Miss Peebs staring down the hall leading to her living room and kitchen.

"I didn't say nothing," Junior said quietly.

"If you'll just be still, you can wait in the hall," Miss Peebs told him. "I will call you." She rushed to the kitchen to make them tea.

Now why did she have to tell me to keep still? I wasn't talking or moving either, Junior thought.

He left the foyer and walked into the hall where there was only a faint, natural light. As wide as a room, the hall was some twenty feet long. At the far end was a round breakfast table with wrought-iron chairs to one side of the kitchen entrance. To the left of the table was the closed door leading to Miss Peebs' living room.

It appeared that Lynora Peebs had taken all her furniture into the hall and piled it along the walls in preparation for moving out of the apartment. But Miss Pebbs was not moving anywhere. The rest of her house looked the same, crammed with furniture on all sides and piled three quarters of the way up the walls. There were paths through the mess from one room to another, with her powdered footprints marking the way. Stacks of newsprint, periodicals and books spotted with cockroach eggs spilled to the floor from warped, dusty bookcases.

Lynora Peebs' parents had been serious collectors of exotic books and musical instruments. They had raised her, their only child, in this same apartment and had willed to her all they had treasured.

"Perhaps owning so much was more than one slim girl could handle," she had once said to Junior's mother.

Maybe one time it was a collection, too, Junior thought, but now it's nothing but crumbly trash.

Junior's mother had met Lynora Peebs during one of her frequent searches for culture. Miss Peebs' collection of instruments, her books, the fact that she was a concert pianist, would have been quite enough to impress Junior's mother. But more astounding than these accomplishments was the fact that for three hundred years Miss Peebs' family had lived and prospered in America. None of them had ever been slaves.

Junior's mother accepted the chaos of Miss Peebs' rooms as the mark of the true artist, even though the filth of the place had always nauseated her.

"Be careful you don't bring cockroaches home with you."

Standing in the dim hall, Junior stiffened as the voice of his mother entered his thoughts.

"It's all your fault anyway," Junior spoke to the voice. "Leave me alone."

Junella Brown materialized in his mind. Her

mouth moved but produced no sound. By rigidly controlling his own fantasy, Junior would not permit her any words to say.

"I got you last," he said softly. He had to smile. "What you going to do about that?"

Carefully Junior moved along the path through the dim and cluttered hall. He stopped a moment to listen.

She says she's destroyed the piano. Miss Peebs wants to keep me out of the living room.

Junior inched soundlessly forward, shivering. He felt chilled. He was never cold unless he was getting sick. And it was true, the confusion of Miss Peebs' rooms made him feel he might vomit. He forced his mind away from the churning of his stomach.

She wants to keep me out. She's got somebody in there who doesn't like music. A relative, living here?

Miss Peebs came through the door at the end of the hall. She looked at Junior coming toward her and set her mouth in a grim line. "I told you to wait until I called you," she said.

"Yes, ma'am," Junior said. "I have to sit down. I'll just go on into the living room."

"We'll have our tea right here in the hall at the table," Miss Peebs said firmly. "You may beat your lesson out on one of the chairs. You may sing the note values in tune as you beat the rhythm, paying attention to the content of the melody as you go along."

"Yes, ma'am." Junior sat down at the table. He avoided looking at Miss Peebs. "I want to play a real piano," he said.

"I've told you so many times," Miss Peebs said. Her black eyes flashed, seeming to beg him.

"Yes, ma'am, Miss Peebs, you didn't hurt that piano," Junior told her, "you couldn't harm it." His tone was nearly a challenge. "It's all right if you've got someone come to visit with you. I know how that is. My daddy, he had a cousin, he told me. And that cousin used to come around to borrow five dollars every time it snowed for more than two hours."

Junior forced a half-hearted smile. The last thing he wanted was for Miss Peebs to think he was minding her business.

A look of warm affection passed between them. Lynora Peebs' hands shook as she tried to pour tea for them. She spilled it and sank down into a chair. Finally Junior had to pour the tea. He was glad to have the chance. Miss Peebs' cups were smooth and fragile, and cool to the touch. Awkwardly, Junior performed the task without spilling the tea.

The two of them sat there, silent for a time. Miss Peebs' hands shook every time she set her cup down. Junior listened for anyone moving around the living room. Whoever might be there surely knew how to keep quiet. Maybe whoever it was couldn't stand a lot of sound, just like his mother couldn't stand it.

Fleetingly he wondered if Miss Peebs noticed that he wasn't beating out his lesson.

I won't do it, he told himself. She is going to have to let me play her piano.

Lynora Peebs sat, seeming to struggle with herself. Every other moment, she looked about to say something but would change her mind. Junior quickly understood he would have to give her time for whatever it was she was trying to decide.

"I told you about the solar system we were making," he said. "Mr. Pool and Buddy Clark. Buddy made a whole new planet. Now there are ten planets instead of nine and the tenth one they made just for me and named him Junior Brown."

Miss Peebs sighed. She shook her head disapprovingly. "Your Mr. Pool has no business keeping you from your school work. You should have no business with a man like that, nor with that boy who waits for you each Friday on the street. Oh, I've seen him," she said, "your Buddy Clark."

"No, ma'am," Junior said, surprised by the meanness with which Miss Peebs spoke. "Buddy knows more math and science. Mr. Pool once was a teacher, see, and he taught Buddy a lot of it. Buddy's my friend. I thought maybe he could come up one time while I have my lesson." Junior was shocked to hear what he'd just said. He didn't know why in the world he'd asked permission for Buddy to come to the lesson and, anxiously, he looked at his teacher. "Buddy could wait in the hall. He wouldn't bother anything."

"I won't have anyone here while you take your lesson," Miss Peebs said.

"That's what we need to talk about," Junior told her. "I mean, how can you call it a lesson? I can't keep on coming here and not even get a chance to show you how I am sounding."

"So few students can become concert pianists," Lynora said. "Perhaps one in a thousand musicians has the gift and stamina for it."

"Mainly I just want to know the theory and composition," Junior told her. "Then maybe I'll be able to teach it in college or something."

Miss Peebs' face twisted in a lopsided grin. "Then you won't need to practice on my piano. It's a concert piano for concert pianists!"

Her smile changed into tight knots about her lips. "I didn't mean that!" she whispered. "Junior, I've been so upset—I do have someone here visiting." She leaned closer to Junior. "I don't know what to do with him since he has no place else to go . . ."

Junior looked around, wide-eyed. He felt frightened to think that somebody might have heard every word they had spoken. "I could get my daddy," he said.

"Shhh!" Miss Peebs whispered. The sound rushed around them.

"I mean, my daddy could come down and help you, if you want," Junior said, as softly as he could.

The bright smile Miss Peebs flashed at Junior was out of keeping with her obvious fear and whispering. "Why, who said I needed your father to come here?" she asked Junior. "You're not to tell your father or anyone!" Glancing toward the living room, she said, "I thought I could nurse him back to health— you know, he isn't well—but he doesn't seem to know or care how bad off he is. Twice when I've been busy in the back, he has slipped out of the apartment. I have no idea how many people he's infected. I do want to keep him in the house until he's well enough to leave. Oh, but I don't know if he'll ever be well."

Junior had long since stopped wondering about Miss Peebs' occasional queer behavior. Being with her in her house was much like being with Mr. Pool in the basement of the school. He didn't have to change himself over to suit either one of them. Neither she nor Mr. Pool ever bothered him about his fat. In fact, Miss Peebs never seemed to notice it.

But now Junior listened to Miss Peebs with a certain amount of disbelief. She had lived by herself since her parents had died. She had been content with her privacy and her music.

"How come you took him in your house?" Junior asked her. Suddenly he felt uncomfortable with the question. "But I guess he's some kind of relative."

"Relative?" Miss Peebs said. One birdlike hand touched her earlobe. She sighed with an odd, shaky laugh. "Yes, and I thought he must have died by now. But here he comes with his socks on strong, pretending he is ready for a fight."

"Would he mind so much if I took my lesson?" Junior said. "Couldn't I go in and play for fifteen minutes?" Junior longed for the sound of the grand piano. His deep-down loneliness would disappear for a while if he could just play it.

"He can't have any visitors." Miss Peebs' voice was cold. "He hates noise. Beat the lesson out on a chair, or on the table. I'll clear it off." She got up, taking their half-consumed cups of tea and the teapot to the kitchen.

Junior's legs felt weak and rubbery when he got to his feet. His insides were churning with a bruising hunger. He walked the short path to the living room. The door was closed but there was no lock. Junior listened. Not hearing any sound, he turned the knob and went inside.

High above Amsterdam Avenue, Miss Peebs' living room faced the scream of fire engines and the rumble of traffic. The closed windows were hung with heavy drapery. Even so, noise seeped inside, became trapped there and lived in the room.

The room was dark and musty. Uneasily, Junior could feel it settle in around him. He fumbled for the switch on the wall and flicked on the ceiling light. What he saw in the pale, yellow glow made his skin crawl.

"I told you to leave it alone," Miss Peebs said. Her crisp voice cut through the noise and narrow light. Not bothering to wash the tea-cups and saucers, Miss Peebs had dumped them in the sink, then had hurried back to keep watch on Junior. She came into the room on the main path as Junior had a moment before. And now she waited behind Junior, her eyes fixed on the folds of Junior's neck rolling over his soiled shirt collar.

Like the entrance hall the living room over-flowed with enough antique and equally shoddy decoration to furnish three households. The main path led past chests, bureaus and the one sofa directly to the front windows facing Amsterdam Avenue. Branching off from it to the right was a narrow path leading to a rear hall and Miss Peebs' bedroom. On the left side of the main path was a perfectly clear, circular area in which sat the grand piano. Its massive, elongated heart shape made all else in the room seem cheap and faded.

The room was a total wreck. Immediately Junior saw that the piano had been the focus of some attack. Vases, cups and dishes, glasses, lay splintered among the piano legs. The piano's rich, mahogany surface had been gouged with some dangerously sharp tool and marked by blows the size of hammer heads. A cup of coffee had broken over the black keys, spilling liquid onto the piano bench. The coffee mess had dried the color of turkey gravy on the ivories.

Miss Peebs' grand piano had been lovely to look at. It was still beautiful to Junior. The many weeks of his concern for its fate came to rest in that one awful coffee stain. His insides quaked for fear the damage done to the piano had gone beneath its surface.

"I told him he would never play it," Miss Peebs said, from somewhere behind him. "When he went ahead, I saw stars—I beat him. Yes, I whipped him about his head and I threw everything I had at him!"

Someone had flung the contents of bureau drawers from one end of the room to the other. Chairs were overturned. A table lay smashed. Junior saw all the damage through the image of the coffee stain.

"Why would he want to play it, if he hates sound?" Junior thought to say.

But Miss Peebs went on, "These are my private things! I cannot stomach anyone searching through my house as if they owned it."

"I can clean it up for you," Junior said. His husky voice came from a great distance. He could not take his eyes from the piano. "All I need is a sponge and a cloth to clean up the keys."

"You must get out of here or you will catch a serious infection," Miss Peebs said.

"There's not a soul in here but us," Junior said, musing to himself. He didn't need to look around him to know that he and Miss Peebs were alone. He heard the soft sound of her footsteps move away to the doorway.

"He's hiding again," Miss Peebs said.

"No," Junior heard himself saying. He turned around to face her. "I think he must have gone out before I got here."

A wan smile brightened Miss Peebs' face.

"You'd better leave then," she told Junior, "before he gets back."

"Can you manage here alone, with him?" Junior spoke carefully. "I mean . . ." he stammered, ". . . not to fight, not to destroy the piano?"

"Not to worry, Junior," Miss Peebs said vaguely. "I'm strong. I'll keep myself busy and not let him annoy me."

"You are going to leave that piano like that?" Junior said.

Miss Peebs became irritated. "I'll clean it—not to worry, Junior. I can come in here now and not let him get the best of me. And I will give you your lesson next Friday for sure."

Miss Peebs smiled brightly. She dismissed

Junior with her blank and feverish eyes. Junior could think of nothing to do but gather his books and get out.

"Next Friday?" he said. He was moving down the entrance hall, away from where Lynora Peebs leaned heavily on the table.

"Yes! Yes!"

"I'm going to bring my friend Buddy or I can't come. I told him he could hear me play," Junior said this stubbornly. If anyone could convince the relative to let Junior play, it would be Buddy. Furthermore, Junior knew he would not step foot again in the apartment by himself.

"Yes, go!" Miss Peebs told him.

Junior let himself out of the apartment. In the empty corridor he shuddered with wave upon wave of relief to be gone. Almost instantly he was on his guard, for in the corridor he was cut off completely from the life within the apartments and the life on the street below. Frantically Junior pressed the elevator button. Beyond the elevator the corridor curved to the right. Junior couldn't help wondering if someone waited just beyond the turn. He thought he heard something.

It's the relative.

Junior made a break for the steps to the left of Miss Peebs' apartment. He went down as fast as he could. By the time he had gone three floors, he realized he had plunged into semi-darkness. The only light was the wan daylight entering onto the stairway at its landing. Each floor had a window overlooking the long shaft between Miss Peebs' building and the one next to it.

What's waiting down on the next landing? Junior thought. He turned on the stairs to start back up again when he was overcome with the notion that whoever had been waiting beyond the curve of the corridor on Miss Peebs' floor was now waiting on the landing above him.

In a blind rush Junior heaved his bulk down to the next floor and hurled himself against the elevator.

Come on! He pushed the elevator button again and again. Keeping his eyes tight shut, he fought back his fear.

Who was it creeping down the stairs from above? In his mind, Junior saw the man's shoes. The shoes were black, the leather so worn it had creased to the softness of kid. The leather had gaping holes slit by a razor to ease the pain of festering bunions. The heels of the shoes had worn away. The man's ankles, covered by filthy silk socks, were swollen and discolored. Behind Junior's eyes, the stench of the man was unspeakable. It was an odor of decay. Junior saw the man's ragged pants cuffs caked with filth before his second sight went blank and the elevator door sliding open

wrenched his eyes wide and clear. The elevator
went down without stopping, carrying only
Junior. The whole time Junior concentrated on
cooling off and stopping the sweat that poured
out of him.

Junior came tearing out of the building. He
swung his legs loosely, his body rolling from
side to side. "Man," he said. He looked up.
The sky was evening dark. Not yet night, it
was suppertime, the end of a working day. It
was a resting, quiet time before the town came
to life again as the city of darkness.

Slowly Junior felt himself grow calm. He
turned this way and that, looking for Buddy
Clark through the crowd of people hurrying
home. Buddy appeared from behind a parked
car.

"It's late, man," he said. He looked at
Junior, not at all disturbed at having to wait
longer than usual. To Junior, it appeared that
Buddy had not been waiting so much as he had
found himself ready to leave at the same time
Junior was ready to go.

"You didn't even freeze yourself," Junior
said, noticing how comfortable Buddy looked.

"I found me this place," Buddy said. "This
some kind of coffee house. Weird, man. I was
talking to this soft little thing who don't know
where she going and can't remember where she
been."

"Sticks like her going to tie you up one day," Junior told him.

"Never happen as long as I keep moving," Buddy said. Already Buddy seemed to be going off from Junior and preparing himself for the time he would have to leave Junior. Junior felt this withdrawal happening as he had before. He accepted it as he did the fact that freedom ended for him once he went home to his mother's house.

"We can take us a bus," Junior said. "If I get on a subway, I'll might be sick."

Buddy looked at him curiously. "You want to ride a bus all the way uptown?" he said. It was then he saw that Junior was drenched in perspiration. "Getting yourself a real kind of cold, man," Buddy told him.

The two of them walked without talking to 79th Street and Broadway. They waited twenty minutes for a bus.

"You going to catch hell from your mother, being so late," Buddy said. "You sure musta had yourself some long kind of lesson today."

Junior searched Buddy's face to see if he were teasing. But Buddy was intently watching the street, part of his mind already loose from Junior. Still he and Buddy were talking easy, in a way they had not spoken for a while.

"She don't care if I'm late," Junior told him. "She only want me to be sure that once I do come home, I don't bring nothing from outside in with me."

The way Junior spoke touched Buddy. Gently he said, "You had yourself a time today, didn't you, man? What happen up there with you and your teacher?".

Finally Junior said, "You won't have to wait outside next Friday." He could see the Broadway bus stopping down at 72nd Street. "Miss Peebs say you can come in while I take my lesson."

Buddy kept quiet. His mind clicked off the pieces of Junior he could put together. Junior had tried to get rid of him every Friday. Now Junior was telling him he could go someplace he never was allowed to go. Junior had been late this Friday. Something had gone on at the lesson. Junior had come out of it not afraid to have Buddy say a little something about his mother.

The bus arrived. After they had found seats together, Junior couldn't make himself tell Buddy what had happened to Miss Peebs' piano.

This relative started messing with Miss Peebs' piano and she had to throw all kinds of stuff at him—how was that going to sound to Buddy? Or, you see, she had this cup of coffee in her hand and she threw it at her cousin and got coffee all over the piano keys. All right. But how do you explain the hammer marks? Did her relative do that just because he hated noise? Or was he vicious?

"How come I can go with you now?" Buddy broke in on him.

It took Junior so long to find an answer Buddy was ready to believe he wouldn't answer at all. But then Junior began to stammer, "You . . . you know . . . Miss Peebs is different . . . you know it better than me . . . some people are different from all other people . . ."

Junior didn't know how to describe Miss Peebs in a way that would explain her to Buddy. The place she lived in would seem like a madhouse if he tried to talk about it.

"She is having some trouble," Junior said. "She's got this somebody, this awful relative who forced himself in on her. She has to let him stay because it turns out he's pretty sickly, even though he can still get around."

"Well, what was he like?" Buddy asked him.

Softly, Junior began about it. "I was so afraid of him." His voice, getting louder, "Oh, man, he was dirty. He stank. He was stinking from his filthy socks!"

Junior heaved himself in a rocking motion, the way a caged bear will sway in a summer's stifling heat.

"Junior, stop it," Buddy said. "You about to knock me out of my seat!" Buddy grew alarmed. People on the bus were turning around. The bus driver kept his eye on them through the mirror.

Abruptly Junior stopped when he realized, like an explosion in his head, that the man he described to Buddy had been someone he had imagined.

"Fool," Junior said, "why do you have to bother me all the time? I didn't even see him. I wasn't anywhere *near* him."

"Then how come you have to lie like that?" Buddy said. "I'm through with you!" Disgustedly, Buddy folded his hands on the seat in front of him and rested his head on his outstretched arms.

"I didn't see him because he slipped out of the house," Junior said. "I didn't want to tell you since she's got to get rid of him. But he ain't just sickly, he's so bad off, he can infect a lot of people."

Buddy sat up, looking at Junior. "You mean, this cat's got a disease so bad, he supposed not to go outside?"

Junior had not thought about diseases. "I guess so," he managed to say.

"And you stayed in that house where there's a cat with a disease and you want me to go there too?"

"I didn't even *see* him," Junior said again, "I wasn't anywhere near the room she makes him stay in." He lied without knowing what he said was a lie.

"You have to come with me Friday," Junior told Buddy. "You got to help me . . . I mean, help her . . . because he doesn't want me to have my lesson. He maybe even could damage her concert piano. . . ."

For some time Junior had kept secrets from Buddy. Now everything was coming out in the open. Still Buddy could hardly believe that Junior suddenly wanted to have him come to his music lesson next Friday.

"Maybe sometime next week I can come see you at your own house," Buddy said. He looked unconcernedly out the window.

In Junior's mind, his mother's fearful presence tried to warn him against bringing Buddy home. By gritting his teeth, Junior was able to hold her back.

"I guess so," Junior said. "I'll figure out a good time when Mama isn't feeling too sick."

"Maybe about Wednesday," Buddy told him.

"And then on Friday, you can come with me to Miss Peebs'," Junior said.

"We straight then," Buddy said. "Nobody going to keep you from having your lesson."

On the bus, Junior and Buddy watched people hurrying along windswept Broadway for fifty blocks. Junior felt safe with Buddy and safe hidden in the seat. Except for hunger which had gnawed a numbing hollow inside him, he had a long, nearly peaceful ride all the way uptown.

4

For Buddy, the city of darkness was deeply familiar and as fine a treasure as any he could have dreamed. He had accepted its mindless indifference to life because he knew it was he, alone, and others, as alone as he was, who gave it what little humanity it had.

There were hundreds of kids like him who had never known what even the poorest home was like. No one worried whether they had a floor to sleep on or food to eat; whether they had got into trouble, or if they were getting along all right. It was not that no one cared about them, Buddy knew. It was simply that no one had any idea they existed.

Rarely did Buddy trouble himself about his mother, whom he hadn't seen since the age of nine. He knew she had abandoned him because his presence reminded her how completely unable she was to care for him. Out of desperation she had walked away from him. Buddy had been glad to never again have to see her suffering. If Buddy longed for anything, it was for a brother. He had known many brothers, but not a single one whom he could run with or just even make angry once in a while.

Buddy recalled living in the hallway and in the basement of the building where he and his mother had lived before she left. People knew him and felt sorry for him. They gave him clothes and some food. Once in a while people would take him in to live with them. But people had children of their own. Just when Buddy thought he was going to stay one place, the children there would fall into a fit of jealousy. The next thing Buddy knew, he was back sleeping in the hallway.

Maybe that was why somebody had called the Children's Shelter on him. He'd barely gotten away in time. He'd seen the car pull up about the time he was bedding down for the night. He'd had to lay there and be cool about it, sitting up, rubbing his eyes when they kneeled over him. They asked him his name and if he had any living relatives. He had taken his time. His plan for escape had depended on his sounding truthful. Buddy had told them his name. And then he first made up the story about his mother really being his aunt.

His mother had left him, Buddy told them. So he stayed with his aunt, who lived over on the next block. But she had told him to get out; she wouldn't even let him take his little sister, who he was afraid would starve. That had done it.

"Where does your aunt live again?" they had asked. He explained and when they took him outside, he pretended he thought they were kidnapers and he wouldn't get into the car. He began to cry. "Just walk around the corner with me and I'll show you where she live," he told them. He threw a fit until finally one said, "We can walk around there, leave the car, we'll get it later. Let's find out about the other child, his sister."

That was how Buddy had won them over. They all had walked around the corner. Buddy had walked in front, planning which building would be the one where his aunt lived. There were three good buildings which had courtyards connecting with buildings on the next street. If he could get on the next street, two streets over from the street on which they had parked their car, Buddy knew he would be free. He could run in and out of buildings so fast, they never would find out which way he'd gone.

Buddy's plan had worked like the charm he knew it was. He had lost them in the maze of tenements in his neighborhood. Only hours later, when he had stumbled into an incredible, new world, did he wonder why he had run away from the only people in the whole city who might have taken good care of him.

"Come listen to my sto-ray . . . Did you ever want a brother?" Buddy made his way down to Broadway and 42nd Street, singing his song as he walked part of the way, or humming when he had to take a subway to keep warm. He had to get over to the Port Authority Bus Terminal, where he kept his things. Close to dawn, Buddy would start making his way back uptown to end up outside Junior Brown's house. But during the night he never once thought of Junior, whom he had seen safely home.

Buddy had to keep his mind on himself and what he was able to do. He avoided walking on Eighth Avenue, where he knew too many people, especially sticks who sometimes followed him around all evening bumming from him what little money he kept for his work. He knew every kind of hustler there was on Eighth Avenue, and his instinct warned him away from those vacant-eyed young sticks walking the streets.

Buddy made his way quickly across Eighth Avenue over to Ninth and then Tenth. He had a place on Tenth Avenue in a boarded-up building that was due to be torn down in some vague future. He had chosen the building with care. The first floor had caved in on the basement. It had been necessary for Buddy to fashion a ladder out of rope, which he used to lower himself into the rubble. He had knotted the rope ends of the ladder tightly around the first-floor cross beam. The ladder hung down into the middle of the basement next to a mountain of debris. Although the upper floors of the building were used occasionally by all kinds of wandering men, never did any of them stumble on the hiding place in the basement.

Buddy entered the building through a window on the first floor, at the side away from the corner. The building next door was quite close and the space between it and the window was pitch black. Buddy felt along the window until he found the loose boards he had crossed in such a way that they could not be pushed in. He uncrossed them and set them on the ground. Then he yanked at the planks covering the window opening. They came out in one piece. Buddy eased himself gingerly through the opening and sat on the ledge inside, replacing the boards and the planks. He could accomplish this feat in about twenty minutes, but there had been a time when getting into the window opening had taken him most of an hour.

Buddy relaxed on the ledge a moment. Beneath his feet was a section of floor extending around a small bedroom for about a foot be-

fore it caved in to make a jagged hole seven
feet across. Buddy gripped the window frame
and stretched his leg straight out. He swung his
leg back and forth through the air until he had
located the rope ladder. He stretched out his
other leg and caught the ladder between his
ankles. After a minute he was able to loop
the ladder around one foot, bringing it back to
where he sat.

Buddy let go one hand from the window
frame to grab the ladder. Leaning back out of
the window so he wouldn't fall forward before
he was ready, he took a strong grip on the
ladder with his hands and feet and swung himself out into darkness. Buddy climbed down
the ladder with his eyes tight shut. He had the
eerie sensation that he was suspended forever
in space, that there was no beginning to the
ladder and no end. Again he told himself as
he had before that there was no need for him
to keep his eyes open and chance dirt and
mortar falling into them.

That's not why I keep them closed, he
thought. Actually he didn't want to be reminded of his blindness in the dark.

I'm not afriad.

It was true, his heart beat steadily and he
was not even breathing hard.

To be afraid of the dark is to be afraid of
Buddy Clark.

Finally Buddy's feet touched the solid base-

ment floor. He eased himself into a standing
position, grunting with relief. His hands were
sore from the hemp of the ladder but otherwise he was fine. He held onto the ladder with
one hand in case he would need suddenly to
swing back up again. The ladder was as in-
visible as he was in the blackness.

Buddy didn't move. He listened, relaxing
one arm and hand at his side. Sounds from outside were muffled here. He could tune them out
of his mind from long practice, so that he was
aware of only sound from the basement. He
heard breathing. Buddy listened to it for a long
time and located it to the front of the mountain
of ceiling mortar and floorboards. Next he listened to hear if the breathing was strained at
all. There was tension in the sound; it told
Buddy that whoever breathed so hard was
frightened.

Buddy smiled to himself and waited for
whatever kid it was to control his fear. Alone
in the city, courage was an important bit of
schooling, for the kid without it couldn't survive long.

There was a scramble of feet around the
mountain of debris to a place on the other side
from Buddy. Figuring out the sound of movement, Buddy knew there were two kids hiding.
He was disappointed in them. He let go of the
ladder. Bending, lifting one foot and then the
other, Buddy removed his shoes and socks.

Barefooted, he walked soundlessly over the icy floor. The rope ladder hung to the right of the mountain of debris. Some eight to ten feet in front of the ladder and the debris was the basement wall. The kids would expect him to come forward from the ladder to the open space in front of the debris. Buddy guessed that they would be crouched on the other side facing front, in the hope of hearing him coming, getting around him and reaching the ladder before he could find them.

They don't know it's me, either. They are going to break for it because they're sure it isn't me.

Buddy made his way around the back of the mountain. When he had taken four steps on the other side, he was directly behind the kids without their having heard him. Inside himself Buddy felt the contentment of his own confidence. In the dark he had taught himself to see with his mind. His senses heard and smelled and registered in him the smallest detail about the boys. And then Buddy crouched and sprung on them, catching their necks in the crook of his powerful arms.

Soundlessly the boys struggled to breathe. As Buddy applied more pressure to their throats, they grew stiff, stunned by the knowledge that they were at someone's mercy.

With a gruff laugh Buddy loosened his hold, flinging the boys away like stuffed toys and then rushing them again to grab each one tightly by the shoulder.

"Tomorrow Billy!" One of them said, "Jeesus, it's you!"

"Is it really him?" the other one said. This boy was younger than the other. Gripping his thin shoulder, Buddy could feel him shaking.

"It's me," Buddy said. He loosened his hold on the younger boy but kept his hand on him. As the boy moved closer to him, Buddy gently held him by the scruff of his neck.

"Okay now," Buddy told them. He kept his grip on the older boy. "Before we move, tell me what's happened."

"Nothing's happened," the older boy said.

"Nobody's come in to sleep or anything, on the upper floors?"

"Nothing," the boy said.

"Please, Tomorrow Billy . . ." It was the younger boy talking against Buddy's chest. ". . . turn on a light . . . please."

"Not yet," Buddy said quietly. "The first thing you must remember is not to hurry with anything. And next, you got to stop being afraid. I know," Buddy said, "it's hard to be cool in the deep dark. But if you remember not to hurry, you'll have time to beat the fear. Now," he said, "just listen."

They listened. The older boy was able to separate the outdoor sounds from their own breathing. His pulse still beat too loudly in his ears so that he could hear little else. Also, he was tired, having had to coax the smaller boy down that rope ladder for half an hour.

The younger, smaller boy could hear only his own ragged breath. He could smell the damp and musty black of the basement but he was not even aware of sound outside.

Buddy heard everything. He captured the sounds of outside and held them in his memory. If they changed at all, if footsteps were added, if any part of the traffic flow at the corner slowed or turned into the street, he knew it.

Buddy could distinguish sound. But he had not known sound at all when he was the size of the younger boy whom he held onto now. When he was that age, about nine, he had stumbled upon a vacant building all boarded up. And climbing to the top floor of the building to escape the people from the Children's Shelter, Buddy had come upon that unbelievable world of homeless children. There had been six or seven young boys and one bigger boy in that boarded-up tenement. When Buddy came upon them, none of them had moved. The bigger boy had been sitting on his haunches, his every muscle ready for battle if a fight were needed.

They all had looked at Buddy. It had been the bigger boy who motioned him to come forward, who had given him a bowl of soup to eat.

"This is the planet of Tomorrow Billy," the bigger boy had told Buddy. "If you want to live on it, you can."

Buddy remembered he had feared the bigger boy at first, even when he had decided to stay. He had been afraid they were crazy addicts, or that the big boy forced the others to steal for him.

The bigger boy had told Buddy, "If you stay with us, you'll do as I say to do. There're no parents here. We are together only to survive. Each one of us must live, not for the other," the boy had said. "The highest law is to learn to live for yourself. I'm the one to teach you how to do that and I'll take care of you just as long as you need me to. I'm Tomorrow Billy."

In the dark of the basement, remembering that time, Buddy smiled to himself. He scooted along the floor, moving the two boys with him until he reached the wall in front of the mountain of debris. There Buddy released them. They moved quietly until they were sitting with their backs against the basement wall.

There was a low table next to the two boys. Buddy found the one patio candle on it and lit it. The weak light seemed suddenly bright to the boys' unaccustomed eyes. Buddy sat on his knees with his palms flat on the table top, staring into the candlelight.

How many Tomorrow Billys had there been, and for how long? It had taken Buddy three years to learn all that the bigger boy on his planet could teach him. Each night, the boy came to where the group lived high up in the tenement. When he had taught them and fed them and furnished them what clothing they needed, he would prepare to leave them again. Always they'd ask him, "Tomorrow, Billy? Will we see you again tomorrow night?" The boy had always answered yes. But one time, after about three years, they'd somehow forgot to ask the question. Tomorrow Billy had never returned. The group had broken up then. Long after each had gone his separate way, Buddy realized why the boy had not returned. It was not that they had forgotten to ask the question, "Tomorrow, Billy?" It was that they no longer needed to.

Turning from the candlelight, Buddy surveyed the two boys against the wall. Their eyes hadn't left his face. He recognized the older of the two to be one of the few kids he had passed along to be part of a group down on Gansevoort Street in the West Village.

Under Buddy's steady gaze, the boy thought to tell Buddy his name. "I'm Franklin Moore," he said. "You may remember me as Russell. That was my real name, the one I had when I first came here."

Buddy laughed inwardly. It was a strange

dude who would change his name from Russell to Franklin. But it was a rule that a boy moving from one planet to another would have to change his name.

"I don't want to know your real name," Buddy told him. "Keep it to yourself, if you need to. But try to forget it, if you're really Franklin Moore."

The boy said nothing. He was quick to learn and his mind clicked in time with what Buddy had just revealed to him about himself.

"Were you told to come up here?" Buddy asked him.

"Tomorrow Billy down there say to come up and bring this kid here because they are full up and you suppose to be just through with one group."

Buddy listened closely to Franklin Moore. The boy could be a thief, stumbling on the group the way Buddy himself had years ago. No. Once you start suspecting them, you'll end by giving them passwords to get in. You'll have to put them in uniforms so you'll know who belongs. You'll next distrust anyone who might forget the password or has his uniform stolen.

"What's your name?" Buddy asked the younger boy. The boy was small and yellow-skinned. His hair was freshly cut and washed and he wore clean clothes.

It took the boy some minutes to come up with a name. He had been taught for however long he had some parent to teach him that his name was who he was.

"Look," Buddy told him. "If you want to use the name you were born with, okay, because I'll never know the difference. See, I can't get inside your head so maybe you make up the name and maybe you don't, it's all right. But dig, it's better you give up the name you were born with. See, because just having a last name the same as the mama or aunt or daddy you once knew reminds you of them. And remembering is going to make you feel pretty bad sometimes when maybe Franklin here or anybody else, either, isn't around to make you feel better."

The boy still hadn't said anything. Every now and then he peeked shyly at Buddy. Clearly he was in awe of his Tomorrow Billy.

"I think maybe he might be hungry," Franklin told Buddy. "We had to do some hurrying. I found him out on the street begging. Some drunk had got hold on him and was making him work for him."

"You have to stone the drunk to get the kid away?" Buddy asked.

"Nothing like that!" Franklin said. He looked shocked but then he understood that Buddy had been testing him.

"I gave him enough money to satisfy the drunk," Franklin said. "When the drunk had his wine, I just disappeared with the kid."

"Good," Buddy said.

"Time we get over to the house on Gansevoort, it's getting late," Franklin continued, "and I know I've got to get him stashed before night. So they get him cleaned up there and cut his hair—but he didn't eat because we had to get up here while I can still see the ladder good enough to get him down it."

Franklin sighed, glancing at the child next to him. He had already grown somewhat protective of the boy. It was always a pleasant surprise for Buddy to see how quickly an older boy became attached to a younger one. Always the younger one would grow up better able to take care of himself than the older one had been.

"I guess maybe you are hungry too, just the same as the kid," Buddy said to Franklin.

Franklin stared down at his hands, fearing his hunger would appear selfish.

"Nothing wrong with needing to eat, man," Buddy told him.

Buddy moved to the edge of the candlelight. In the shadows there stood a double-door file cabinet. Buddy unlocked it and opened it; there were stacks of clothing on the upper shelf and a supply of towels and soap. Canned goods, staples, plates and cooking and eating utensils were kept on the two lower shelves. On top of the cabinet were quarts of bottled water and a Sterno set.

Buddy lifted down the Sterno and water and set them on the table. He took from the cabinet a can of soup, a loaf of dark bread, powdered milk, two bananas and a can of tuna fish.

The boys watched eagerly as Buddy spread the food out on the table. "Yea!" he said happily. The boys scooted forward to help.

Opening the bottled water was like a ritual. The younger boy was allowed to do it. When he had used the opener properly in order to get the bottle top off, he leaned back, satisfied.

From a drawer in the table, Buddy produced three small paper cups. "Now," he said to the younger boy. "You'll pour a half a cup of water in each of the cups. You can drink it that way or you can mix it with milk. If you mix it with milk, you can have more if you want. But if you have only water," Buddy said, "you can have just a half a cup. We buy the water, so it's precious in the wintertime with all the water fountains turned off."

The younger boy would have his water mixed in with milk so he could have a second cup. He poured out the water, clutching the large bottle tightly in both hands. When the task was done, he forced the top back on the bottle. He passed the bottle to Franklin, who, when he was finished, passed it on to Buddy. Buddy returned the bottle to its place on top of the file cabinet.

They ate tuna fish sandwiches. They had hot soup followed by banana slices. All of the food tasted wonderfully good.

Softly the younger boy spoke. "I got a name for myself," he said.

Buddy was chewing, so he didn't say anything. The boy stared up at him with wide, happy eyes.

"So what is it, what's your name?" Franklin asked.

"Nightman," the boy said.

There was a dead silence, after which Franklin said, "Naw! That's not a name!"

"How come it's not?" Buddy asked him, for the younger boy had looked crestfallen. "Take a name like Malcolm, Malcolm X. Now that's an opinion when you think about it. But a cat's got a right to his opinion."

"Well, is Nightman a first name or a last name?" Franklin asked the boy.

"It's a first name," the boy told him. "My name is Nightman Black."

Buddy had to smile at the kid. The kid had made peace with the dark by making himself a part of it. "That's a good, tough name," Buddy told him. "Nightman, you are real together."

After the dishes were cleaned and put away, and the cabinet locked again, the three of them

sat against the basement wall. Buddy talked
quickly but calmly to the two boys. He spoke
particularly to Nightman Black. It would be
hard for him to catch on at first, Buddy told
him. Nightman would naturally go to the sec-
tions of town where there were black people.
That was all right so long as he stayed out of
bars, so long as he kept himself moving. Don't
stand on street corners, Buddy told him. The
best place to rest was in playgrounds but only
at lunchtime and after three o'clock. He
wouldn't be going to school for another week
or two. Buddy told Nightman that he couldn't
go to school until he was safe being on his own.
Because until he could get by, he would be
nervous. He'd want to go home with the first
teacher who was nice to him. Nightman might
blurt out the fact that he didn't have a home.
He might tell some kid that he had to sleep in
a broken-down building. No, Nightman had to
get behind living for himself; and when he
could do that, he would have no trouble in
school or anywhere else.

"How long do you say I have to travel with
him?" Franklin asked Buddy.

"Just a couple of days. He should know
enough by that time."

"Because I got to go to school," Franklin
said. "When I'm out, they start checking up."

"Where do you go?" Buddy asked him.

"Down on 81st and Amsterdam," Franklin

told him. "I'm doing good, too, and I don't want to miss no school!" He spoke flatly, angry that he had to have Nightman tagging after him.

Buddy looked out on the mountain of debris in front of him with cold, solemn eyes. He'd had a feeling about Franklin from the time he'd lit the candle and had begun questioning the boy. Now all his knowledge of the street and its people came together in certainty.

Without turning his head or moving the trunk of his body, Buddy reached out, grabbing Franklin by the throat. The movement was so swift and casual, Franklin was pinned down across Buddy's lap before he knew what had happened. His throat ached from the pressure on it as Buddy searched his pockets, inside his shirt and down in his socks. What Buddy found, he flipped onto the table. When he had a pile, he let Franklin sit up. Buddy held Franklin tightly in a hammer lock and forced him to face the table.

There were two expensive gas lighters, both gold-plated. There was a jeweled wristwatch and two diamond rings. There was an onyx-handled knife with the price tag still on it and a black leather wallet.

Buddy reached over to check out the wallet. It was full of money, about seventy-five dollars' worth, and credit cards. There was a receipt for a rent-a-car.

"You ain't nothing but a thief," Buddy said, "a wet-bottomed little hustler." He shoved Franklin against the wall and got up with the wallet in his hand. "There never was a school at 81st and Amsterdam!" Buddy added. Unlocking the cabinet, Buddy searched for and finally found a torn piece of paper and a pencil. From the cards in the wallet, he wrote down its owner's address on the paper. He had no envelope and no stamps so he would have to wait until later to mail the stuff to the guy.

Buddy counted the money again, then took twenty-five dollars of it. He put back the remainder of the money, placed the pencil and paper in the wallet's fold and stuffed the wallet inside his jacket.

Buddy's mind went quiet. He had caught the slightest sound and he was moving toward the rope ladder before he had turned himself around to face it. He caught Franklin before the kid had started up the ladder.

"You didn't think you were going to make it!" Buddy said. "You know you can't get out of that window fast enough."

Buddy lifted Franklin away from the ladder and hit him hard across the face. Franklin shuddered. The slap had jarred him to his toes but he made no sound. Slowly he walked back to the basement wall and sat down beside Nightman.

Nightman sat with his mouth open. The look on his face was one of dread. Buddy hated seeing the fear in Nightman's eyes. Now Nightman knew how trapped he was. He knew that if Buddy wanted to hurt him, there was nothing he could do to stop him. But without panicking, Nightman sat where he was, for he had discovered that his life depended on Buddy. He had learned how dangerous it was to be small and weak.

Buddy placed two tens and a five-dollar bill on the table. He picked up the five and gave it to Franklin. "For you," Buddy told him, looking him in the eyes. "You use that for whatever will do the most for you and Nightman in the next few days."

Stunned, Nightman sucked in his breath. He looked from Buddy to Franklin and back to Buddy again. "You're not going to make me go —you're not going to make me steal with him!"

"See what you've done?" Buddy said to Franklin. The boy looked down, turning his head away from them.

"Tell Nightman you won't steal," Buddy said, "and don't come on with how this is the first time. I'll break your arm, man, if you come on with how you haven't ever done it before."

Franklin turned angrily to Buddy. "You just now stole yourself twenty-five dollars," he said.

He shook with triumph. "You ain't nothing but a thief yourself."

"I took some money out of a wallet you stole," Buddy told him. "I took only enough to give you all a chance to make it until Monday when I get paid."

Buddy was tired, for it had been a long day. He was taking too much time here and he had to have it over with quickly now. "Nightman," he said, "Franklin is going to show you how you can take from this town just enough to get you through each day as it comes around. Every morning you're going to wake up hungry and with nothing. By the evening, you'll be hungry again and with nothing. But before dark, you bring yourself back here and wait for me. When I get here, you'll eat."

"You still got yourself some twenty dollars," Franklin said, "not even counting the wallet with the rest of the stuff. Why you need it if you going to get paid on Monday?"

Buddy studied the boy a moment before bringing his shoes and socks from the other side of the debris. His feet were aching from the freezing cold. Hurriedly he pulled on his socks. They were cold and filthy, stiff with dirt and sweat. He slipped into his tennis shoes.

"I'll mail the wallet off when I can find an envelope and some stamps," Buddy said. "But I need the twenty dollars. Not for myself, though, but for kids like you two who maybe will need it." He paused. "You don't have to believe me."

"I don't," Franklin said.

There were some kids, Buddy knew, who you never could like and Franklin was that kind of kid. Buddy was so used to the younger boys doing exactly as he told them. The safety of the planets depended on the trust the boys had in their Tomorrow Billys. But Franklin didn't trust Buddy because he was untrustworthy himself.

You have to work with him, Buddy thought. You can't turn him loose. With what he knows, he could come down on all the planets. He could take his time cleaning them out one by one of what little they had. Then if the Billys got rough with him, he could blow the lid on them. No, you had to turn him around and get his distrust working for you.

"You want me to put all the money in the file? You want me to put the twenty dollars back in the wallet and mail it back to the cat it belongs to?"

Franklin struggled with himself. Even if he was a thief, he had been with the planets long enough to have a heart for the lost kids. He wouldn't take a few dollars away from them. But how was he going to be sure this Tomorrow Billy was straight?

Buddy could almost hear Franklin's mind clicking. He won't be able to work it out,

Buddy thought. How will he, when he can't even trust himself?

"How about you, Nightman?" Buddy said. "You want me to put the twenty dollars back in the wallet?"

Nightman was frightened. He could look at Buddy but he couldn't bring himself to look at Franklin. But beyond the fear in Nightman's eyes, there was something dark. "I want you to put back the five dollars you give to Franklin." Nightman laced his fingers together and searched his palms. "All I need is an apple or an orange and maybe a roll for breakfast and I don't need no food again until suppertime."

"You think you won't," Franklin told him. He had the five dollars deep in his pocket. He wanted to keep it there. "We can't come back here until nighttime and you going to be sniveling crying for some hot food way before then."

"I never cried for no food yet," Nightman said. "I maybe don't like being in the dark but that's because I haven't learned about it. S'nothing scares me about the day . . . give him back the five dollars."

Reluctantly, Franklin pulled out the money. Rather than give it to Buddy, he slapped it down on the table. "There," he said to Nightman. "I ain't going to be responsible for your starvation."

"What do I do with the twenty, Nightman," Buddy said, "and what about the wallet?"

"Well," Nightman began, "I believe you when you say you going to mail that wallet back to the man. Because I want to believe . . . because I got no reason not to. And for the twenty, I think you better keep it for the others. I don't imagine you need it for nothing."

How come one boy was so different from another when they both hurt the same? Buddy wondered. "That all right with you?" Buddy asked Franklin.

Franklin looked around at Nightman, who sat with his legs folded in front of him, a hand on each knee. If Nightman had had a throne, he couldn't have looked more like a king.

"Just like he say," Franklin told Buddy.

Buddy moved away from the boys, placing the rest of the items Franklin had stolen in the file cabinet. Behind the file were metal folding cots slung with canvas. Buddy motioned Nightman away from the wall. Franklin followed. When both boys had moved, Buddy set up the cots. Each cot had its own sleeping bag, which Buddy shook free of dust before spreading it out on a cot.

Thoughts flew in his head as he worked, making the planet ready for the night of darkness. Is this all there is to it? he wondered. I'm to be a nurse for them and a teacher of lessons, like in Sunday school. I know my Tomorrow Billy was different. I just can't seem to remember what it was that made him different.

Buddy left the boys. He blew out the light and stood in the dark a moment. Franklin was on the cot on the outside and little Nightman was against the wall and deep inside his sleeping bag.

The place was so quiet and the boys so still, no one would ever guess they were there.

Buddy turned toward the rope ladder when Nightman said sleepily, "Tomorrow, Billy?"

Buddy grinned in the dark. "Yes," he said. Then, he climbed up through blackness. Taking his time, he swung the ladder when he was level with the window. He got outside with hardly a sound. Replacing the boards firmly over the window, Buddy enclosed the boys far below in night.

Outside Buddy found the city of darkness awake and full of action. Buddy wouldn't have known it any other way. Bouncing on the balls of his feet like a fighter, Buddy made his way to the Port Authority Bus Terminal. He ducked in a side entrance to avoid the regulars—the homeless old men and women who waited for a chance to slip in and sleep for a while on a bench. It was getting hard for them to find a place to rest in the terminal, for the night patrol regularly passed through to keep them moving.

Instinctively Buddy took on the appearance of a traveler. Maybe he was a young soldier going back to Fort Dix over in Jersey. No, he didn't have a duffel bag or anything. Maybe a student, going across the river after a night in the Village? Buddy decided on some combination of the two. He knew he didn't need to be clearly one kind or another. He had merely to look as though he had a destination and he knew perfectly how to look like that.

In the terminal Buddy strode to the cigarette machine and bought a pack of long filters, although he rarely smoked. Carefully he opened the pack and lit a cigarette. Calmly, without glancing around to see who might be watching, he walked over to study the board listing arrival and departure times of buses. When he seemed to have the schedule fixed in his mind, he nodded to himself. He sighed and hurried over to buy a newspaper. He glanced at the paper briefly while walking toward the restrooms.

So far Buddy had acted his part to perfection. People noticed him—ticket agents, travelers—with that momentary interest people in cities reserve for one another. In one sidelong glance, they had discerned that Buddy was going someplace. He was black. He looked to be maybe eighteen or nineteen but maybe he was younger. He wore tennis shoes. He had a paper, he was smoking and he was sober. No trouble. Just a black kid going home after working in some kitchen somewhere.

I am harmless, Buddy thought. I am nothing at all.

Near the restroom Buddy found the locker where he kept his soap and washcloth. He lifted out the brightly woven knapsack in which he kept all his belongings. Any other time Buddy would have taken longer, the way he liked to. He would have touched the knapsack gently, feeling the bright threads with the tips of his fingers, the way some folks handle old photographs which represent the best of their lives. But tonight he had to hurry. The time was nearly midnight. The morning newspapers were thrown from the delivery trucks by two o'clock. Soon after he would have to be at work.

One moment Buddy was standing in front of the locker, shoving his knapsack back in it, and the next moment he was gone. He might have melted into the stream of people heading for the subway or he might have gone to line up for a bus. So adept was he at taking on the mood and pace of any group of people, it was hard to tell where he had disappeared to. But he had cleared his mind of everything save the object of his intention. He made no mistakes because he allowed himself no anticipation of trouble. Even when Buddy was in the pay shower, he concentrated solely on the hot water beating down on him and the cleansing aroma of Fels Naphtha soap.

Afterward Buddy changed into clean underwear, socks and a clean shirt, which he had taken from his knapsack. He rolled up the soiled clothing in the shirt he'd worn before the shower and stuffed it inside his jacket. The whole time he thought how good it was to be by himself. He was lucky he was strong, with no sickness anywhere in him.

Outside of the Port Authority, Buddy dropped the new pack of long cigarettes at the feet of one of the old drifters and was gone before the man could mumble a thanks.

Buddy strode eastward, allowing his tiredness to slow him down just a little. He was chilled now after the shower. The weather was quite cold this night and he would have to see about getting himself a warmer jacket, maybe a plaid job with a pile lining. Buddy grinned. He could almost feel the fake fur encasing his arms in warmth.

Oh, man, that would feel so good!

Buddy was glad that the night before this one, there had been nobody but himself on his planet in the abandoned building. He had gone to bed about ten and had slept until it was time to go to work. Tonight he would get no sleep.

Between 59th Street and 102nd Street, Buddy dropped his clothing off at an all-night laundry and stopped at two more planets. Each of the planets had a full house but both Tomorrow Billys were broke. Buddy listened to the story of the second Tomorrow Billy, alert to the Billy's calm sincerity.

"The work is drying up," the young man was saying. "I can't even pick up a bus boy job anymore. Students are moving in on us, man. I got to feed these kids so I guess I'm going to have to lift more food than I usually do."

There was danger in stealing too much, Buddy knew. "How are you for sweaters and stuff?" Buddy asked the Billy.

"I got nothing left, man, but some long-sleeved polo shirts," the Billy said. "They not going to keep nobody warm, either. I been thinking about making capes out of the sleeping bags but then I figure the kids would stand out wearing something like that."

"All I got is ten bucks," Buddy told him. "I already give ten tonight to another planet—wait." Buddy reached inside his jacket, remembering he had concealed the wallet there. For a moment Buddy was afraid he had lost it, but no, he had it. He pulled out the wallet and telling the story about it in one long stream of words, he gave the Tomorrow Billy the whole sixty dollars.

"Let me write the cat a note," the Billy said.

"Yea?" Buddy said. The two stared at one

another, their thoughts working over the idea.

The Billy produced a pen. He took Buddy's piece of paper and wrote on it:

*We sorry about the bills but we need im
ta feed the kittis. So, be cool. You a real
dude. We not touch you credit cars. So
dig. Thanks.*
                    A member of the planet.

Buddy and the Tomorrow Billy studied the note for a long time. It looked fine. There was nothing in it that could give them away. The Billy had an envelope. Buddy addressed it and sealed it, giving it back to the Billy to mail.

"You got a crowd over where you are?" the Billy asked Buddy. He was a dark-complexioned, tall and thin fellow with soft, happy eyes.

"Just only two," Buddy told him. "I got finished with a group of them about a week ago but it took them all that time to figure out how I wasn't coming back. But they cleared out, finally."

Buddy spoke softly. This planet thrived in the busy meat-packing area isolated from the huge industry farther downtown. Refrigerated trucks could be heard all around them. They were in a small, dank warehouse room virtually sealed off from the rest of the enormous building by the use of plasterboard, paint and movable wallboards fixed over the door. Still, the planet wasn't as safe as it could have been. Buddy and the Tomorrow Billy talked of this for a moment.

"I already studied it," the Billy said. "There's a place down near the Brooklyn Bridge I found out about. We going to make it over there by late Tuesday night."

"How will I find you?" Buddy said. He liked this Billy. He wished he could ask him about the things he did on his planet.

"I can send somebody over about Friday to bring you down," the Billy said. "I maybe will send you two or three boys besides, if you can take them in."

"I can take them in," Buddy told him. "You do that." But that was all. His nagging notion that he should be doing more on his own planet he kept to himself.

"Later," Buddy said. He was gone, melting from the dark room into the hall. Outside he skirted the trucks. Staying in shadow, he was a black movement under cover of night. Buddy slipped away. By three o'clock he was uptown.

Buddy stopped once for a cup of coffee at 102nd Street. The coffee tasted foul and left Buddy moody and jumpy. He had walked the rest of the way to his job, reaching the news-stand long after his legs had begun to ache. The stand was a lean-to built on the side of a corner apartment house. There was a food shop and a men's wear store on the ground floor of the building facing Broadway. The lean-to took up the space against the building around the corner from Broadway, on the cross street. It had a rectangular opening on the side street, like a peepshow, with magazines, pamphlets and digests hanging on all sides and neat stacks of daily papers on its counter.

With his last strength Buddy heaved bundles of morning newspapers thrown from delivery trucks onto the sidewalk through the side door of the stand. With cold, stiff fingers he knelt down to unwind the wire which held the bundles tight. Buddy felt pleasure in having hands whose strength could untie metal knots.

The man sitting behind the counter of the newsstand facing the street didn't turn around. He was Doum Malach, Buddy's boss. Doum was twenty-four years old and out of college. He had inherited the stand from his father, who had retired. Doum wore his usual long, army surplus coat and a black velvet beret. The outfit looked like the military uniform of some exotic country and gave Doum Malach a look of distinction. As far as Buddy knew, Doum belonged to no organization and he made a fair living off the newsstand.

"If you had some sense, you'd use a wire cutter," Doum told Buddy. He still did not turn around. "Go on, tear up your hands, they're good for nothing no how. Hurt your own self, go ahead. Leave a whole town full of crazies with nothing to bleed."

Buddy grinned at the back of Doum's head. "Good morning, Mr. Malach," he said. "I see you woke up feeling good this morning."

"Don't call me mister, I told you. And furtherwise, I haven't been to bed, clown."

"Hey, Doum, you got any coffee?"

Doum Malach swung around in his swivel highchair. "You got the price of fifty cents a cup?"

"Come on, man! I haven't done nothing to you!" Buddy told him, "I had a lousy cup on the way up here and I can't get the taste out of my mouth."

"Up here from where?" Doum said quickly. He stared at Buddy with interest. In the months the kid had worked for him, he could never figure out where he lived or from which direction the kid arrived. Buddy was simply there one minute and gone the next, never giving up a clue.

"Up from seeing a stick down on 95th Street," Buddy said evenly. He reached up to get the wire cutter from a tin can on the counter, then dropped to his knees again.

"You're a liar," Doum said. "You're a secret Olympic swimmer. You a test pilot for the glider corps. Maybe you're a rock and roll singer that's lost his voice. Who are you, anyway, clown?"

"I'm a lost, secret, rock and roll test pilot— hey, come on, Doum," Buddy said, "gimme some coffee."

"Gimme some coffee, gimme, gimme, that's all you've got to say. It's all anybody's got to say, just gimme, with nary a thank you or never mind. Didn't anyone ever tell you, ol' Buddy, that Don't Care Don't Have No Home?"

Doum fixed Buddy's coffee in a heavy cut-glass goblet. He made it black, with plenty of sugar, just the way Buddy liked it. The coffee aroma filled the space between them, so much so that Buddy couldn't tell anymore whether it was Doum he cared about like a brother, or whether he loved most the good coffee Doum fixed for him each early morning.

"My mother always said that," Doum told Buddy, handing him the steaming goblet. "She say, 'Go on, disgrace your poor mother, Mister Doum. And if I never tell you nothing else, I can tell you this, fool, *Don't Care Don't Have No Home.*'"

Doum threw back his head and laughed. Buddy watched him, sipping his coffee.

"She throw you out before they give you the grant of money to go to college?" Buddy asked him.

"Long before that, man," Doum said. And

then he stopped talking. In the light of the street, his face was suddenly veiled. "Why should I tell you something?" he said. "You don't tell me nothing."

"I got nothing to tell," Buddy said. He could feel himself reaching out, wanting to open up with Doum, but he didn't dare. What could happen if he told Doum about the planets? Doum wouldn't know where they were. Even if he found out, he would know to keep his mouth shut.

You never can tell, Buddy thought. A cat can seem one thing just like I do and be something altogether else.

Buddy stood to put his goblet down on the side of the counter, right behind the place where Doum kept his gun. He was careful not to touch the weapon; and never questioning the need for it, he wondered again if Doum ever used it.

Buddy put morning papers in neat piles on the apron outside the counter. He placed new magazines on clips hanging above the counter. He pasted the most startling magazine covers to the sides of the stand, arranging them with all of the calculation of a designer. When he had finished, Buddy stepped back to survey his work.

Doum sat leaning out on the counter, noting that it had taken Buddy close to forty minutes to arrange the covers. He knew Buddy took his job seriously and he never teased him about the time it took him. "How's it look this Saturday morning?" Doum said.

"Looking all right, I guess," Buddy said. "But somehow, they all are using dark shades for their covers, the browns and greens and stuff and it all comes out kind of gray."

"We have us here a period of unrest," Doum told him, "a time of caution and camouflage."

Buddy came back inside and sat on a cushion on the floor to one side of Doum. In that position he could see Doum's profile. Doum could talk to him without turning away from the street.

Buddy fixed himself another cup of coffee. "What's good to read?" he said. He didn't like to leave the stand before six o'clock. He had himself plenty of time.

Doum handed him a cheap-looking blue pamphlet with red lettering at the top. The letters spelled the words, *Free America*, which was a quarterly and high-priced at fifty cents.

"Shoot," Buddy said, "give me something with some pictures. I don't feel like no close reading."

"Read the poem on the back," Doum told him.

Buddy turned the pamphlet over. He saw an ink drawing under the poem. This black figure was sitting hunched over, a scraggly bird picking at its scalp.

Buddy read the poem but he didn't care for it. It was about turning in guns you might own to the cops and the cops wouldn't ask you any questions about where you got the guns in the first place. Buddy recalled that sometimes the library would let you bring in books you'd swiped or forgotten about and never asked you to pay for them.

The poem ended in a way Buddy didn't understand. He questioned Doum about it.

"Maybe it's over your head," Doum said. "You see, it's caution and camouflage masquerading as irony—you know what is irony?"

"No," Buddy said.

"Well, it's to say just the opposite of what you mean. Like, the man takes everything you own and you say, 'thank you very much.'"

"So what about the poem?" Buddy said.

Doum explained, "The poet says, go ahead, turn in your guns but come the fight and you don't have a gun, you going to be dead."

"Is that what's known as propaganda too, sometimes?" Buddy asked him.

Startled, Doum stared at Buddy. "It's irony," he said flatly. "*We are all human beings. All men are created equal*—that's propaganda." Doum grimly smiled and flung about six glossy picture magazines down at Buddy, then turned back to the street.

Buddy picked a magazine and read it slowly, savoring every clear, colorful picture. He'd love to one day make the kind of photographs you found in magazines. Buddy read and read, paying no mind to Doum, who had started his endless argument with the street.

Slowly the town turned into the city of light. The street with Doum's newsstand was beginning to look tired and ragged but not at all dangerous. Often people got off buses and stopped at the stand for their morning paper. Or they came up from the subway off their night work and bought the *News.* After they'd gone, Doum told them off. "You can't read, anyway. You wasting your pennies, clown. Tell you anything, you believe sand is brown sugar if it said so in a headline. Mellonhead, nothing but pulp and water for a brain . . ."

Buddy was so used to Doum's fussing talk he could close it out without thinking about it. After a couple of hours of reading, Buddy slipped away. Doum didn't hear him go. He had been quietly reciting a play he had memorized, acting aloud all the lead roles while saying the minor parts to himself. As the sun rode low over Broadway, Doum was well into the second act, his voice purring words and his hand making delicate drum taps on the butt of his revolver.

With sunup, Buddy's night-being seemed to rise out of him. He had climbed into a cross-town bus before he realized he had begun a second life. Buddy found himself on his way to

Junior Brown's house and he gladly gave up his knowledge of darkness for adventure.

Junior Brown! Man, we can spend maybe two or three hours up in Inwood Park and then cut back to 42nd Street and the library.

By the time Buddy had planned their day, he was off the bus and on Junior's street. He recalled how Junior had been late getting home after his piano lesson.

"Hope he didn't get into too much trouble," he said softly.

Across the street from Junior's house Buddy rested his back up against a building. He looked questioningly over to the other side of the street and up three stories to the windows of Junior's apartment. He stayed in that position for nearly two hours. Ever so slowly, excitement left him. His face fell in resignation as he realized Junior wasn't going to come down. It was then Buddy remembered Junior had told him his father would be home way early in the morning this Saturday instead of Saturday evening, which was the usual time he came home.

Buddy stayed for a few minutes more; then he turned around, going back the way he had come. This time he walked the long city blocks, stopping to rest when he had to but always continuing on. He didn't go to Inwood Park, nor did he go to the public library. Half dragging himself, he went to the basement

room of the school. The basement hallways
were still as tombs as he passed silently along
them. In the secret room Buddy didn't bother
to turn on the power of the planets. He
stretched out on the floor under them, com-
forted by them and the steam heat of the room,
which warmed the dark. Instantly Buddy's
eyes closed. He dreamed nothing. He slept the
whole day.

On Saturday morning Walter Brown didn't
stand there at the threshold of Junior's room.
Half asleep, Junior knew his father wasn't
there.

"Daddy," he said, because he wanted to.

His father might have come in the room
wearing his robe and slippers and freshly
creased slacks. He always did come in to
Junior in a warm, respectful manner, as if
Junior's room were the chapel he had known
all his life. Usually Mr. Brown entered Junior's
room at night. This morning might have been
different. They could have had the whole day
before them.

"Daddy," Junior said again. His voice was
husky with feeling. "I haven't seen you on a
Saturday morning in forever."

Junior reached up and rubbed his hair.
There was a breeze up there, it felt like, blow-
ing through his scalp and lifting up the top of
his head like a lid. At once he had a huge

and terrible hunger. Then his mother came swooping in on him, pulling at him. Opening drawers, she found his clothing for him. Straightening chairs, his mother bothered the room into near human retreat and suffering.

"Junior," she said, "you and I will just have to share the day between ourselves."

"Then Daddy's not coming at all," Junior said. He knew all along.

"Your breakfast is fixed so get your clothes on," she told him.

"What do I get to eat?" Junior said. He had a suspicion, like a bad taste.

His mother tried to get out of the suspicion by being sweet to Junior.

She said, "I've made you some coffee. You can have milk in it but no sugar. There's cereal and milk, with peaches—fresh peaches —sliced on it. There's toast. I cannot allow you to have butter on the toast."

"I want some eggs and bacon and hot rolls and pancakes."

"No."

"Mama, I'm so hungry."

"Get up," she said to him.

Junior sat up on the edge of the bed. His mother helped him into a clean shirt, manipulating his heavy arms as though they were lifeless hams, first one arm and then the other. She gave him one-word directions. "Lift. Move. Turn. Lift."

She had Junior dressed in a few minutes. Junior made his own way into the kitchen while his mother stayed behind to order his room. When she returned, she found Junior had prepared his own breakfast. He had six eggs on a plate in front of him. He had cooked a mound of bacon placed next to the eggs.

Junella stared at the bread she had toasted for him. Junior had spread it with butter and a thick layer of jelly.

Junior wolfed down the food, eggs first, in oozing gobbles. He consumed everything he had prepared, every bit of bacon and all of the toast his mother had made.

Without seeming to notice, Junior saw every look, even the slightest movement of his mother watching him from the doorway. He loved his mother. He had this toy he had kept for a long time, he didn't know why. You wound it up and it would do the same thing over and over until it wound down. You wound it again and always it would do just what it only could do. Like his mother. Junior always knew she would do the same things over and over. There was safety in knowing that.

He loved his father. At fifteen and a half, his father had walked out of the Big Black River country of northern Mississippi. He had taken one last look at the rich and bloody river-bottom soil and had headed into sandy foothills of scrub piney woods. His daddy told him, by the time he had walked across a third of the state and into Tennessee he was no longer a boy. He had become a man who ever after carried with him the scent of Mississippi danger.

Slowly Junior started eating the cereal his mother had wanted him to have. He ate it all while staring at her and willing her to sit down. She did come and sit down right next to him at the table. She gathered her skirt in around her. She crossed her legs under the table. She folded her hands in front of her and cast her eyes down to one side.

"We can go to a museum," his mother told him. "We can go to the park. It's cold, but we can walk around. Junior? Try to believe I'm sorry. I thought he was coming home. Maybe he'll come home by tonight. No. Don't even think about it. No, just don't get your heart set again."

Junior could hear movement, televisions, in other apartments, so still were he and his mother. He could hear the street; and beyond their street, other streets. The city out there was loud and bright. All of it revolved around Junior like a wheel, like a system in an immense spiral. Junior knew he was the center and the point of it all.

He commanded the system to halt. A thunderous roar was the city stopped. With the crack-up of the last corner, Junior was left with the kitchen. His mother hadn't moved or made notice of ended sound. She was caught there in time with him. She dangled in rhythm with him drinking his coffee. Junior knew the fire-chord which could make her spin and dance. He played one red tone at a time. Their street crackled, other streets kindled. The city flamed and lived.

"Buddy Clark might be waiting for me to come on down and spend some time with him."

"The boy has gone and left you," his mother said.

"Why didn't you wake me?"

She shook her head rapidly, as if to dis-lodge cobwebs. "You needed your rest," she said.

Junior's hunger lay curled like a warm ache from his core. He burned from a great distance. He was a lonely star.

5

This Monday morning was no different for Buddy than any other Monday. He was by himself and ready for the day. He had slept all day Saturday and all day Sunday. Saturday night he had looked in on Nightman and Franklin and had taken care of them the way he knew how. The boys were getting along together. Nightman was developing a keen eye. He had found a fantastic spindle of green butcher's string in an alley.

"I make out how it must've fallen offen a truck," he told Buddy. The spindle was cream colored, huge and heavy, and made from wood. The green string was wound on it half a foot thick.

"Man," Buddy told him, "I bet that spindle is some kind of antique. I bet some antique shop in the Village would pay good money for it."

Nightman had looked shocked, clutching the spindle tighter in his arms. He wouldn't allow Franklin or Buddy to touch it. "I found it, so it's mine, isn't it?" he asked Buddy.

"It's yours," Buddy told him, "if you can think of something to do with it. Otherwise it's dead weight and useless. We'll have to sell it for the money. The string ain't worth a thing."

Nightman studied the string, touching it with his hands. Finding the string end, he unwound some of it, lacing it through his delicate fingers.

"I know it's good for something," he said. "Now if I could just think what could be that something."

"Let's set a time," Buddy had told him. "Let's say about Wednesday."

"A time for what?" Nightman had wanted to know.

"When you have to think of something else or I will sell the spindle for the money."

"Let him have until Friday," Franklin had said. "Give us some time to look around and see what we can do with it."

"We won't do anything with it," Nightman said, "because I got to do it all by myself."

"You can have Franklin help you, it's all right," Buddy told him.

"I do it by myself, or you can have the whole thing right now," Nightman said. Stubbornly he had clutched the spindle of string. Then he thrust it toward Buddy.

"You keep it," Buddy had said. He had pushed the spindle back into Nightman's lap. "You keep it and you figure out what to do with it all by yourself."

Buddy had not seen Junior Brown for the whole weekend. This Monday morning he didn't feel like going by Junior's house, he told himself. So he went on to school alone. When he arrived in the basement room, he found Junior already there and Mr. Pool there, with the solar system full of juice and turning silently through the void.

Not so silently. There was a piercing squeak somewhere, a high scraping sound like metal grating against metal. As the planets revolved, Mr. Pool tried to pinpoint the squeak. When he thought he had it, he turned off the solar system. He pulled a ladder over and set it up by the planets. The he climbed up and cleaned all of the tracks from which the rods were suspended.

"There. That ought to do it," Mr. Pool said when he was finished. He shoved the ladder away into the void and turned on the solar system. The squeak remained.

Buddy laughed. He came around the planets to where Junior was slumped in his folding chair. Buddy didn't say anything; he just stood quietly behind Junior's chair. This way he let Junior know they were together. And together they both watched the system.

The planet of Junior Brown soon became a giant presence in the darkness. The solar system became all and mighty in the void. Except for the squeak.

Mr. Pool's bald head glowed yellowish in the light of the system's dim reflection.

"Damn it all to glory!" he muttered. "It's got to be up in the tracks."

Buddy told him, "You ought to let the master of sound tell you where the squeak is. Meaning Junior," he added. He leaned to one side, peering around Junior until he could see Junior's face. "Good morning to you," Buddy said. "You have a nice weekend with your daddy? U-huh? You and your daddy eat in some big-time restaurant and see some two-dollar technicolor movie?"

"Cool it off now," Mr. Pool said to Buddy. He had heard the anger in Buddy's voice. It had surprised him, but when he thought about it, he supposed Buddy's anger was there in almost everything Buddy did.

"So Junior's father took him some place," Mr. Pool said. "You don't have a father to give you things—is that it?"

Buddy let himself go loose. He collapsed on the floor, on his stomach, half in the light of the solar system. "No," he said. He turned away from Junior and Mr. Pool to rest his head on his arms.

He was tired. Why in the world did he have to say that to Junior! He only meant to let Junior know that he understood how Junior had to spend the weekend with his father. He was tired down to his bones. He had walked around a good part of the night again—that didn't make this Monday any different from some other. But the night and this early morning was colder; he had to keep every muscle working to keep from freezing. Buddy knew he would have to steal a warmer jacket and he was tired of stealing.

Way early this morning, old Doum Malach had given Buddy his pay. Thirty-seven dollars and fifty cents.

Buddy grunted to himself. The grunt sounded like pain to Junior. Mr. Pool had heard it too. He came around the revolving planets to where Buddy lay half in darkness.

Thirty-seven dollars and fifty cents, with some kids coming up to his planet next Friday from someplace down at the Brooklyn Bridge. He would have to find warm clothes for them to wear. He would have to get them cleaned up, and enough food, Jesus, all on thirty-seven dollars and fifty cents.

Again Buddy grunted with the deep-down worry of it.

"Are you all right, Buddy?" Mr. Pool stood

over Buddy, wondering if the boy maybe was going to be sick.

Suddenly Buddy felt strange, like he was coming down with something.

All I need is to catch me a sneaking pneumonia.

"You want to set yourself down?" Junior spoke. Since he had entered the room, Junior hadn't said a word. He had wished for so long to be able to say things to his daddy, but he never had his daddy to talk to. It was only Buddy he could tell things to. Buddy had to be the one. "You want to sit down here?"

Junior pulled his chair over closer to Buddy. Buddy looked around and then got to his feet.

"Naw, man," he said to Junior. "You sit on down like you were. I'm just getting myself warm."

"Well, how you feeling then?" Junior asked him.

"I'm feeling fine. I'm just a little tired, that's all," Buddy told him. "I meant it serious though," Buddy said, "when I ask you did you have a good time this weekend—did you?"

Junior stood there with his hands folded in front of him. His legs were slightly bent, as though they weren't quite strong enough to hold his bulk. He shook his head. "It wasn't much of a time," he said.

Mr. Pool retreated to the far side of the solar system to let the boys talk. As the planets spun by him, he touched them with the very tips of his fingers and waited.

"Why wasn't it much of a time?" Buddy was asking Junior.

"It just wasn't," Junior said. He sat down in the folding chair once again. Buddy moved closer to hear. "He never did come home," Junior said.

"Aw, man," Buddy said, "I was up there too. When you didn't come down, I thought sure . . . All that weekend by yourself!"

Junior felt like he might cry all of a sudden. "You got to go with me on Friday," he said. "Buddy? Right? You promised you'd go with me to my lesson on Friday."

"Okay, okay, don't I always go with you?"

"I mean, go in with me so you can see for yourself. Will you go in with me?"

"I promised you, didn't I?" Buddy said. He didn't remember any such promise. "Look, man, don't get yourself all upset. I'll go with you. Everything's going to be fine."

Junior let his breath out in a ragged sigh. "This coming Wednesday I'll take you over to my house," Junior said. "I promised I would and I will."

Finally Buddy remembered the bus ride when he and Junior made their deal. "You sure your mother won't get mad at you for bringing me home?"

"You'll come over," Junior told him, "and

my mother won't be mad that you can see."

Waiting, overhearing, Mr. Pool smiled to himself. It had taken Junior Brown all this time to admit to himself that he needed Buddy Clark, that he could go no further with something he had to do without big Buddy helping him.

Maybe that's a beginning, Mr. Pool thought. He knew about Junior's mother. She was a self-centered, sickly woman who was probably good at heart. It upset him to know she would condemn Junior's friendship with Buddy simply because Buddy looked tough.

She isn't going to like one bit Junior bringing a poor boy home with him.

The squeak of the solar system intruded on Mr. Pool's thoughts.

"Somebody help me find that squeak," he said, touching the planets.

"Maybe the squeak isn't in the system at all," came from the far side of the planet. Buddy Clark.

"It is in the system," Mr. Pool told him.

"But maybe the system is just rubbing too hard against the dark," Buddy said. He laughed loudly at his own nonsense.

"Keep it down," Mr. Pool said. "We're going to get ourselves caught because of you."

On the far side, at the edge of the void, Buddy covered his mouth. He'd forgot for a moment that the solar system was not somehow

up in space. He was feeling better. Here he was
going over to Junior's house on Wednesday,
just like some regular cat, and then on Friday,
he'd go over with Junior to see Junior's music
teacher. He'd straighten everything for Junior
with the relative. Buddy was cool, whatever
was wrong, he could fix it. Maybe soon he and
Junior would be really tight, like brothers.

Like somebody I can tell everything to, even
tell about the planets.

Buddy looked at big, bad Junior sitting so
sad in his chair.

Man, when you see what I am into—taking
care of kids, working my job. Wait till you
meet old Doum—man, blow your mind! You
going to want to be free as me . . .

Tuesday was no different and Wednesday
Buddy lay on his back in Junior's room. He
tried to remember when he'd rested on anything as comfortable as Junior's bed. Buddy
had to keep blinking his eyes to keep from
falling asleep. Junior's room was so peaceful.
The heat of the house poured into him, warm-
ing him to his soul.

Junior played the piano across the room
from Buddy. He hadn't been practicing much,
he told Buddy earlier, but today he had felt
like playing. As the windows filled with winter
shadows, Junior played on and on.

Filling Junior's mind was the swelling, bursting sound of Miss Peebs' grand piano. With the strength of his imagination, he tried to fuse the music to the silence of his own Baldwin upright piano. As he pressed the soundless keys, he thought the responding tones. He never could quite imagine them as pure as the music of the concert grand.

Buddy watched Junior with amazement. For Junior swayed like a dark, brooding bear to an unheard rhythm in the stillness.

Since he'd come into the room, Buddy hadn't believed what he was seeing. Several times he couldn't help heaving himself up from the bed and tiptoeing over to the piano.

The top of Junior's piano had been taken off so that more sound could get out. But all of the wires meant to vibrate to make that sound had been removed. In place were the felt hammers made to hit the wires when the piano keys were pressed down. But the hammers struck against nothing. As Junior played on and on, the hammers rose and fell senselessly.

Buddy turned over and pressed his face into the soft fabric of the bedspread.

He felt empty of himself but outraged at the damage done to Junior.

Taking away his sound from him, Buddy thought. How could she do that to her own son?

From some far place, a deep place of his heart, Buddy slowly understood.

All their lives, they have been this family, he thought. Up so close, and for so long, they can't separate any of it. She has to have rest. Junior has to play his piano. I bet that's the way it is.

Buddy sat up on the edge of Junior's bed. He watched hulking Junior swaying in time with silence.

He plays a piano without sound and she has her peace and quiet. "God Almighty," Buddy said out loud. He got up.

I can't stay here anymore.

"Junior? Hey, man? You finish up so we can split someplace. You want to see a film?"

A minute passed before Junior stopped. Smiling, he rubbed his hands together, as if he were washing them. He grinned at Buddy while his eyes remained sad. "A movie?" he said.

"Anything," Buddy said. "Let's just get out of here."

"I never do go out at night," Junior said.

Buddy stared at him. "You just went out the other night, a week ago. I saw you," Buddy told him.

"I never go out without my mother," Junior said. The grin quivered.

I'll swim the river before I take his mother to a show, Buddy thought. "Man, you can go with me if you want," he said. I might even show you my planet. How am I ever going to get you down the ladder to see it? Maybe if I just tell you about it, we both could figure a way to get you down there. "You got to want to go," Buddy said. "Man, it's up to you."

"I haven't had my supper." Softly Junior spoke and got up from the piano.

"Nobody said it's ready yet," Buddy told him.

"Nobody has to say," Junior said. He stood with his hands folded in front of him, his head down, as though he were praying.

Buddy didn't realize at once that Junior was waiting. By the time he did, Junior's mother had walked in on them. She came close to Junior. She held her hands folded in front of her the way Junior did.

"Your supper is ready now, son," she said. Mrs. Brown turned to Buddy. She stiffened, her thought bristling with contempt. Buddy Clark towered over her the way her own son would not. Hard with muscle, he was over-bearing even when he was not moving or speaking. "You are staying for dinner, of course," she said to Buddy.

"That was the plan me and Junior had," Buddy said right back at her.

Boldly, Junior's friend was staring her down. She knew any decent boy would have lowered his eyes. But she continued to study him as though he were some rampant thing too widespread to be destroyed. He was not too

different from the growth she weeded from her
window box. And if she ever had the garden
she dreamed of, she would cut this Buddy down
toward evening.

"Come along then," she told him. Buddy
waited for Junior to go first. Then he followed,
ashamed he hadn't found the nerve to tell
Junior's mother what he thought of her.

Buddy never did know too much about the
inside of people's houses. He had only a few
vague memories of such places. The homes
were dark, walls were bare and moist with
grime. Always there was one table, maybe two
chairs. A bed set in the center of the room
away from rat holes. There was listless quiet,
or noise, coughing sickness. Buddy kept hold
of the memories because they were what he
had.

Junior's house brought back no memories to
Buddy. He saw a nice sofa and a couple of
easy chairs as he passed through the living
room. The dining room was in an alcove off
the kitchen. The walls of the room were
papered in a design of gold weave. A big table
had a yellow tablecloth on it and high-backed
chairs all around it. Carved candlesticks on the
table had tall candles burning in them. The
table had been set for three people. Next to
each dinner plate there was a smaller one. And
above the dinner plate there was still another

small plate. There were cloth napkins the color
of the tablecloth. Besides having a knife and
spoon, each plate had three forks next to it.

Buddy was about to be nervous. His insides
fluttered; he put his hands in his pockets, then
awkwardly down at his sides. But something
bright washed over his brain. In one sweep of
his eye over the vivid table he knew how much
care had gone into arranging it. He knew that
on this Wednesday night in the middle of the
week, with nothing better to happen than the
coming of Thursday, the table had been set for
a holiday supper. This was to be the Thanks-
giving or the Christmas feast, or maybe even
just the Sunday one before the time Junior's
daddy went away again.

No. This time Buddy was to be the occasion.

Junior's mother came from the kitchen
carrying a platter of roast stuffed turkey. She
next brought gravy and sweet potatoes, broccoli
and hot baked rolls.

No, Buddy thought. It's not a big turkey,
but it's turkey just the same. You eat it. I am
it. She's going to slice me up and help herself
to my guts. She's going to suck my bones. She
thinks so.

Thinking like that helped Buddy feel calm.
Instinct born in him gave him an inkling of the
man he would become. Some inbred notion
told him that a table was no more than wood

put together a particular way, no matter how you dressed it. The highback chairs were only more of the same. They could have been boxes, it didn't matter what they were as long as you could sit on them, with some surface to put your food on so you wouldn't have to eat in your lap.

No. Sitting down to a spread like this has to make you feel good. Good as anybody. Without it you can't feel half as good.

Silently Buddy stood across the table from Junior. Standing beside her chair, Junior's mother was between them at the head of the table. Buddy could feel her eyes on him. He glanced at Junior to find Junior again waiting for something.

The food steamed up over the table in a mixture of delicious smells in the candlelight. The aroma curled around foreknowledge in Buddy's mind. Easily he moved around the large table to Junior's mother. He pulled the chair out for her and gently held it as she sat down, pulling it in to the table.

All this done in a moment and in silence. Junior sat and Buddy sat down.

Expertly, Junior's mother carved the stuffed turkey. Talking all the while, she said, "I learned carving from my father and his father. My own husband was never home, you see, so learning to do for myself was necessary—

Junior, you may pass the sweet potatoes and gravy. Buddy Clark, begin the broccoli around, please. I expect you are used to the turkey wings, the bony parts—shall I give you the back? Which do you prefer?"

Buddy had served himself a large portion of broccoli and had passed it over to Junior. He had two sweet potatoes neatly on his plate, then spread a small amount of gravy over them. After that he turned to Junior's mother. In the moment he kept her waiting, instinct came to him. Buddy said, "No thanks—if there's giblets in the stuffing, I won't have any of it, either."

Mrs. Brown was caught with the serving fork in the air, ready to puncture the back of the turkey.

Junior grinned at her. "I'll take what he don't want," he couldn't help saying. His mother served him nearly a quarter of the bird and a wing portion with a mound of stuffing. She took a small amount for herself.

"I expect you are some sort of Black Muslim," she said to Buddy. "Pass me the sweet potatoes, will you please?"

"I just don't like eating off any flesh," he said, placing potatoes and gravy near her hand. "It don't seem right somehow."

Junior had filled his fork with glistening thigh meat and skin. He looked at the meat a long moment before he put his fork down.

"Nonsense," Mrs. Brown told Buddy, "A fowl or animal is not 'flesh' at all. It is meat meant to be eaten."

Buddy knew what he wanted to say. He could make Junior's old lady throw up right in her plate if he wanted to. But there was Junior sitting across from him, about to die from hunger, unable to eat because he had called the meat flesh.

Buddy swallowed hard. "I know it's just some kind of problem I have," he said. "I know I should eat meat—no reason not to."

Mrs. Brown smiled, buttering a roll. "I expect your mother finds meat to expensive to buy," she said.

"My aunt," Buddy said. "My mother's still down in Texas." Old lady, see *you* scrounging in alleys. You'd know meat only could slow you down. Break away fast, and meat's going to stick in your side like a knife.

"It's nothing to be ashamed of," Mrs. Brown said. "True, we sometimes fail to appreciate how much we have." She glanced at Junior. "My own father always did say that whatever one had was a blessing." She looked at Buddy. "We have plenty of meat here. Please feel free to help yourself."

In spite of herself, Junella Brown had a feeling for this son of the poor, this stranger in her house. Pity eased into her heart as she reminded herself how he would rather not taste the turkey than have to long for it sometime when he couldn't get it.

"Go ahead," she said. "Believe me, we have plenty."

Junior's mother breathed through her mouth. Buddy had seen that when he first met her but now the fact stuck in his mind.

Fool lady, Buddy thought, see you cut up in pieces. Let some air in. Fry you and see the skin pop. Burn!

"I'd appreciate some water," Buddy said. There was nothing at all to drink at the table.

"Goodness," Mrs. Brown said, "of course you can have some. I never thought, since Junior seldom has anything with his dinner." She got up to get Buddy some water from the kitchen, her breath strained, winded, as she walked away.

"I hate water," Junior said when his mother had gone.

"I'd hate it too, if she was my mother," Buddy couldn't help saying. Rage stung in his throat.

"She being nice to you," Junior said. He looked sullen and guarded.

"Wouldn't want to see her when she's being mean," Buddy told him.

Junior stared at him. "Never mind," Buddy said. "You want to go to a film or not?"

Junior's mother came in with a tray. She

handed Buddy a glass of water. "I forgot the salad," she said. Buddy said he didn't want any but Junior had some. There was apple pie for desert. Junior had two slices. Buddy drank the water, gulping it, not caring about the sound he made. The water cooled him off inside.

Junior's cheeks bulged with pie. His mother eyed his hunger, her face feverish and damp. She saw that Buddy Clark had not eaten his roll, although he had cleaned his plate of vegetables and gravy. She sighed to see so much leftover food. Better to put it away now before Junior became hungry again. She knew she would be short of breath before she had the dishes done.

"Junior and me want to go see a movie," Buddy said. "I'll see he gets home safe."

Slowly Junior's mother began to clear the table. As she worked, going back and forth to the kitchen, she commenced to wheeze. Midst muffled coughing she managed to load a pile of dishes and silverware in her arms, and lurched into the kitchen. The dishes clattered in the sink. At once Junior was heaving himself out of his chair. Still chewing, he moved toward her bedroom. A moment later Junior returned with a bottle of medicine and an oxygen mask.

It all happened so quickly, like a crazy,

speeded-up film. Buddy was standing, not realizing he had got to his feet. He hooked his thumbs on his pockets and held himself utterly still inside. Always he could silence feeling when instinct told him death was stalking. Mechanically he gathered small plates neatly in his arms, while hearing as in a dream the muffled sobs of Junior and the choking of Junior's mother.

At the sink Buddy washed turkey grease from his hands. Junior's mother was sprawled helplessly in a kitchen chair. Junior had hooked her arms through the ladder back so she wouldn't fall to the floor. He had attached the oxygen mask to a silver cylinder he had rolled from a kitchen closet. He shoved the mask over his mother's nose and mouth and held it there. With the other hand Junior released a valve on the cylinder. There was a hissing sound as the oxygen surged, rushing to bring back life.

Buddy had seen Mrs. Brown's discolored face. He knelt beside Junior and took her hands in his. Her hands were no longer warm. Contact with their lifelessness made Buddy wince.

"She's choking to death," Buddy said. "Junior, take off the mask, she's choking."

Splashed with tears, Junior's face looked as though someone had sprinkled droplets of water on it. His body quivered with minute tremors. His hands were steady.

"The mask stays on until she can cough up the sputum. Here," Junior said to Buddy, "hold it for me."

Buddy reached to hold the mask in place. He had to press hard on the mask to keep his fingers from jumping.

Carefully Junior took a gleaming hypodermic syringe from a black box on the table. Buddy hadn't noticed the box until Junior opened it. Junior attached a long, hollow needle to the syringe and then sunk the needle into the bottle he'd brought from his mother's bedroom.

"She's a junkie," Buddy said. He couldn't believe his eyes.

"No," Junior told him. "Needle used for other things, mainly asthma."

"What's the stuff in the bottle?"

"Epinephrine," Junior said. "Sometimes I use it in the needle and sometimes I let her inhale it from a nebulizer." Junior had taken his mother's arm, finding the large vein below the forearm. Buddy knew better than to ask him questions now. He watched as Junior rested his thumb lightly on the needle's plunger. He saw the needle pierce the vein in one sure thrust of Junior's hand. Junior's thumb pressed down on the plunger. Buddy turned his face away.

By the time Junior had cleaned and put
away the needle, his mother was no longer
choking. She began to cough into the mask.

Alarmed, Buddy turned to Junior. Junior
turned off the oxygen. As though she were a
rag doll, Junior tossed his mother toward the
sink and then was there to prop her up before
she fell. His mother gagged and brought up a
mass of sputum over the dirty dishes. That was
all. The siege ended; Junior held her like a
doll, dragging her to her room.

Junior and Buddy cleaned the entire kitchen
and dining room. With no trouble, they worked
together—they were both so used to being
careful and to silence. For an hour they hardly
needed to speak; when they finished, the two
rooms were spotless.

In his room once more, Junior sat on the
piano bench facing Buddy, who sat on the
bed. Junior's face was innocent, like a child's
could be. He did not plead for anything from
Buddy. In his mute exhaustion, he told Buddy
how it was he had to live.

Buddy got to his feet. Junior swung around
until he was facing the piano. His dark,
brawny hands, swollen with flesh, arched skill-
fully as he pressed the keys. Swaying, and
with his eyes closed, Junior played the music
he alone could hear.

"So that's all, then," Buddy said.

Junior heard Buddy but it was hard for him

to listen and hold the music steady at the same time. He could feel heat rising in the core of him, where he kept his fire. He waited to flame.

"It's my fault your mama got sick," Buddy said. "She .went to all that trouble fixing that turkey."

"She won't ever mind cooking," Junior heard himself saying. "She always manage to make a nice dinner."

"Anyway, I'm sorry," Buddy said. "I didn't have to come—I made you bring me here."

Music grew distant. Junior's hands fumbled with the keys. His hands ached with muscles too taut and he had to stop playing a moment. Some halfhearted need took hold of him. He recalled how much of a friend Buddy was. He and Buddy were together. He had no one else to be with. Junior remembered, he took care of his mother but he cared about Buddy. He cared about music—Miss Peebs.

Junior said, "I got checkers. We can play some, if you want. You can take the black. When me and my daddy play, I take the black and black always wins."

Buddy thought about playing. How could they play a game after what had happened?

"I haven't played checkers in a hundred years," Buddy said. He didn't know whether to go or stay.

"You don't ever forget how to play them."

Junior left the piano to get the game from his desk.

"Why is that?" Buddy asked him.

"Because you learn it when you're so young," Junior told him.

"How come you so sure I learned it?" Buddy said.

"You learned it," Junior told him. "Somewhere, sometime, you had to learn to play checkers."

Buddy had to smile. He and Junior sat on the bed with the checkerboard and the box with the checkers between them.

Junior had placed his red pieces before Buddy had half the blacks arranged.

"How come you so fast?" Buddy said.

"Why you so slow?" Junior said.

Buddy said, "I was thinking about when I learned to play checkers. I couldn't have been more than four or five."

"With your dad?" Junior asked him.

Buddy had this vague feeling, almost like night and shadow. He recalled a figure of a man, laughing, playing with him. "Must have been my dad," Buddy said. The memory sank into forgetfulness.

"Down in Texas, where you were born?"

"Must have been," Buddy said.

They played the game. Buddy couldn't get in the mood of it. In the middle of it Junior went to see if his mother was feeling better. When he came back, he sat down again on the bed.

"She all right?" Buddy asked him.

"She's sleeping," Junior said. "She'll sleep real hard like that until morning."

They played. Black won the first game and the second.

"You want to play another?" Junior asked Buddy.

"Not if black's going to win again," Buddy said.

"What you got against winning?" Junior asked him.

Buddy got to his feet. "If I'm going to win altogether every time, there's no fun even playing."

"Black always wins," Junior told him. His face broke into a wide grin. He shook with laughter.

"Why you want me to win every time?" Buddy wanted to say. Instead, he said, "Okay, I'll play another game if you take the black."

"I can't take the black," Junior said. "I'm always red because I'm fire." He laughed in stitches, shaking the bed, his big hands hitting the board and overturning the checkers.

Buddy stared down at Junior. Junior sat there, his arm outstretched on the board and black checkers squeezed tight in his fist.

To Junior Buddy's eyes were glinting pins,

then one steel needle darting out to go right
through him. Junior imagined Buddy's eyes
were telling him he was a mama's boy.

"Why don't you just come on out with me
and leave her?" Buddy had to say. "You not
supposed to take care of her the rest of your
life. Your daddy's supposed to."

Junior moved. He threw black checkers at
Buddy's eyes as hard as he could. He was up
off the bed with his fists swinging. Buddy was
too swift for him—he knew that fighting was
living and breathing. He had brought Junior to
life.

Buddy had whacked the checkers away to
the floor in a motion so fast it had ended
before Junior saw it. Buddy had Junior's flailing arms pinned behind Junior's back before
Junior realized Buddy had got behind him.

"You so smart," Junior said. "Think you're
so tough." With one great heave Junior lifted
Buddy onto his back and shook Buddy off
again over his head. Buddy landed, tumbling
over his own head onto his shoulders and then
on his back. He barely had time to get one
hand in position to protect his neck as he went
over. As it was, he had to lie still until air
seeped back into his lungs.

"If I sit on you, I'd crush you like stepping
on a worm," Junior told him.

"Man, don't sit down on me!" Buddy managed to say. He had to laugh, he couldn't help himself. "Whoo! Man! You got me that time!"

"Get you any time I want," Junior said, "s'long as I'm red—talking about my mother."

"Ohhh!" Buddy said, holding one shoulder. "Yea, that's right. I did hit on your mother. Yea, okay, you're red, all right."

Junior collected all of the scattered black pieces, and with the checkers on the bed, put them in the box. He put the game away in his desk, then stood by Buddy as Buddy slowly got to his feet.

"I have to go," Buddy told him. "I got to get out and walk around."

"You going to see a movie?" Junior said.

"Maybe I will. I got to go."

"You going to wait for me downstairs in the morning?" Junior asked him.

"If you want. Sure." Buddy turned away from Junior, heading for the door.

"I thought maybe you was mad at me," Junior told him.

"You took me fair and square, I'm not mad," Buddy said, and added, "I know you can't leave your mother like she is."

"Remember, on Friday," Junior said.

Buddy remembered. "Don't you have enough to worry over without thinking about that Miss Peebs?"

"You promised!"

"Okay, okay." Buddy's head ached. He wished he'd never said he'd go with Junior to Miss Peebs' house. This one night of people's houses was enough worry to last him forever. "So tell your mother I'm sorry she got sick," Buddy said. "Maybe you ought to get yourself some sleep, Junior."

Buddy went out, leaving Junior standing in the middle of his room. Once outside on the street Buddy looked up and he thought he could see Junior still standing there.

The poor boy, he thought. He was feeling so old now. But the air was crisp and fresh. The night of sounds and lights brushed over him, cleansing him.

Oh, man, it sure is good to be out.

6

Junior was red under his skin. Standing in the middle of his room, he rocked from one foot to the other, swinging his heavy frame from side to side. His fat careened and rolled around him. He kept his eyes tight shut in order to know blackness within which he was red.

Junior's swaying became rhythmic. He did a few turns of a dance, bobbing and flailing his arms. He performed an intricate routine with his feet, sliding them, then quickly stepping and turning. Junior had seen the slim black kids work their feet. He could do it just the way they did it, with his eyes shut, when he could be red.

"*A'm lookin' forty mile,*" he sang. "*Shuh, b'lieve a'm fixin' ta die . . .*" Junior held his wrists close to his belly. His elbows pumped at his sides and his fat hips swiveled, rippling the flesh beneath his clothes:

"Shuh. Shuh. I knew I was bound to die, Cluney,
But I hate to leave my children cryin' . . ."

Junior could dance. Ah, he was a dancing
fool. Cluney was his partner and she could
dance real good. But Cluney had no weight on
her. She was a black stick. She had black rod
legs and arms; she had no red on her at all.

"A'm a low-life clown, with ma head on upside
down, Cluney-Cluney.
Livin' ain't worth even the buyin'
But I hate to leave my children cryin' . . ."

Baby sticks were sobbing all over the place,
so Cluney took them and split.

Junior opened his eyes to the soft light of the
room.

"If I went out for a little while Mama
wouldn't even know it." Junior sat on the floor
next to his desk, by the closet door.

"But if she should almost die, I would be the
cause." Junior knew his mother would never
really die. If she ever did, she wouldn't be able
to blame him.

His room was all over silence, and filled with
the odor of silent dancing. Some silent cotton
curled in Junior's hearing, making a hum in his
ears. The cotton silence had taken over the
sound of his electric clock on the desk. Junior
looked at the clock. It told time but it made

no sound, since its sound had been taken up.

Junior thought, I'm tired of separating sound from things.

For a moment he was one whole self. He knew he spent too much of his time taking out of things whatever substance could identify them. He could take meaning out of words so that words were left brittle and empty. He could take the ring from a phone; he could leave the phone dead and keep the ring buzzing, tickling his palm.

Junior looked at his clock and wished he could leave things alone.

How come Buddy was so free all the time? How come he could go to a movie or just walk around? Buddy had it all free and didn't even see that the people out there belonged to Junior. Buddy had taken what had been free in Junior's house when he went away. He had taken the noise and left Junior with the quiet room.

Don't do that, Junior thought. You are taking things apart again. Oh, why can't there be somebody to talk to?

He was certain that because he was so black and ugly, he was alone.

I got the whole world of noise inside. I'm red inside.

There was nothing for him to do but draw it. Junior opened the closet and took out his paint box and his roll of canvas. The roll was a five-foot width and just the length Junior needed. Spread out on the floor to its length, the roll fit between his bed and desk.

Junior sat with his back to the closet, facing the entire room. The room was a rectangle, with the windows at the far end from him. The bed was to his left, his desk to his right and his piano next to his desk, to the left of the entrance.

Junior reached inside his desk drawer and took out a child's wooden hammer. The mallet end was covered with masking tape, which concealed a lead weight. Junior took the hammer and four upholstery tacks and hammered down the four corners of the canvas as quietly as he could. He put the hammer back in the drawer and closed the drawer. Only then did he relax back against the closet door. With his paint box in his lap he surveyed The Red Man.

Junior had oil-painted a large figure of a man on the canvas. Outlined in black, the figure was seated with his arms behind his head and with one leg crossed over the other. The figure was completely red except for his feet. Junior had left his feet unpainted to show that the red color came from the man's brain. In fact, the skull covering the brain was a throbbing blood-red, darker than the rest.

Junior worked on the figure whenever his mother became ill and he was left to himself for the whole night. When he first began the painting, he had meant only to draw a rod like one of those he had worked with as a child learning math. The Cuisenaire Rods of his childhood were different lengths and colors in units of one through ten. Rods of the same color were the same length. The white rod was one and the orange rod was ten. Ten white rods were the length of the orange rod. Two white rods were the length of one red rod. Red was the unit two. Junior had drawn and painted a rod in red paint because the red rod of his childhood had been the only rod whose color he could always guess with his eyes closed, while holding a handful of rods behind his back.

Gradually Junior's painted red rod developed arms and legs, a head. It still had no facial features but it had become a man. One day Junior would fill his Red Man with people. All of the people would be an inch high, in colors and combination of colors that Junior could mix from his paint box. He had already started painting in people who lived in The Red Man in their apartment houses, on streets.

Junior had The Red Man's neck and one side of his chest filled with figures. From a distance these figures of people and the way they lived looked like the detailed pattern of muscles and veins found in medical books. Or they looked like fine tattooing, with the blue and red colors outstanding and the blacks and browns like pockets of darkness.

Up close, it was clear that The Red Man housed inch-high people of all shapes and colors living their lives.

With his paint box in hand Junior crawled up the canvas to The Red Man's knees. He opened the box and took out a small bottle of turpentine, his flat, square piece of wood for mixing colors and the instrument he used for a paintbrush. Junior had not found a paintbrush small enough to make tiny people and yet stiff enough to outline them and reveal them in detail. He had finally hit upon the idea of using the calamus of a bird's feather. The hornlike stem was hollow and would hold enough paint to etch two figures.

The smell of turpentine and oil paint rode on the silence in Junior's room. Junior opened both windows overlooking the street. He went to the bathroom. Later he looked in on his mother, whose room was next to his, before settling down on the canvas. His mother slept a drugged sleep. To Junior she didn't look like much of anything, lying there, unable to order him. Junior had drawn her a few times in The Red Man. He would draw her again, just the way she lay so fragile on the big bed.

Junior worked with just the sound of his

scratching calamus. The silence soon teemed with his ideas and poured out in an unbroken line from his hollow horn. Junior had thoughts and dreams, which he drew. He had pianos with splendid sound which he painted. He had the school and the planet of Junior Brown. He had the streets with Buddy Clark free and tough, knocking his way through them. He had everyone flowing free—Mr. Pool and his daddy and Buddy's daddy and games and buses and old people and trees. Junior came to paint Miss Peebs and he had a time keeping his hand steady. He had a terrible time with her living room and her piano. That relative!

Junior's hand shook with a palsy but he drew in himself and then painted Buddy Clark between himself and the relative.

No. He scratched out Buddy. He thought of blanking himself out with black paint. Junior did that. He painted himself out in black and he would have to wait for the black paint to dry. He worked on the other side of The Red Man, away from the scene he had nearly created. He worked on The Red Man's left shoulder and forearm until he was too tired to move his hand, until his eyes stung from paint fumes and such close focusing.

Junior cleaned his calamus with a soft cloth damp with turp. He put his equipment away. He took up the tacks holding the canvas down, then slid the canvas under the bed to hide it. He waited to see if the canvas would roll up, but from his hours of lying on it, it stayed flat.

Junior was too tired to put on his pajamas so he stretched out on the floor with the light on, his arms covering his eyes. Junior let himself go loose. He fell asleep long after Buddy had visited his planet and had gone on to work for Doum Malach.

Not very much later Junior's mother came into Junior's room. She looked weak, yet rested. She grew alarmed as she stood there. First she thought Junior had rolled out of bed but then she saw he hadn't even got out of his clothes. She smelled faint odors of paint; she saw that the windows were open and knew Junior had been painting sometime during the night. Junella shivered, for the room was cold. Softly she smiled at her sleeping son, convinced he had stayed up most of the night to watch over her. She left him to make his breakfast and was grateful when she found her kitchen cleansed of horror.

On Thursday morning Mr. Pool got himself into trouble. Junior and Buddy saw it happen. They were lucky they got to the school when they did—just before the homeroom bell rang and after most of the kids and teachers were assembled in their homerooms. Mr. Pool and some man from the maintenance company which serviced the school were standing right outside of the basement door. With that man there, Junior and Buddy couldn't take a chance cutting on out. There was nothing for them to do but go on up the steps and inside the school.

The man and Mr. Pool were arguing. They heard the man say something about how he never could locate Mr. Pool when there was work to be done. The man said it hardly mattered that Mr. Pool made up the time in the evening. They needed a janitor during the day when things went wrong, and they never could find Mr. Pool when they needed him.

"We are wide open and we've got to go in," Buddy told Junior. "We sure can't take a chance going down into the basement room."

"You mean, we've got to go to class?"

"There's no other way," Buddy said. "You just keep yourself cool and do what I do."

"I don't think so," Junior had to say. "I can't make it, not today."

Junior and Buddy had come up walking fast from Amsterdam. They had their books as they always did, like they planned to go to class. Buddy had been waiting for Junior when Junior came out of his building. Junior had looked the same as he did any other day except, when he came out, he hadn't known what to do or where to go. He didn't recognize Buddy until Buddy came over and took him by the arm.

"How you doing this morning?" Buddy had said. "You feeling all right?"

"Not so good," Junior told him.

Buddy hadn't needed to ask. He'd known Junior must have stayed awake the whole night.

"You cool it, then," Buddy had told him. "We'll go down to the basement until just before lunch. Then we'll go on downtown to the library."

"I don't think I can make it," Junior had told him. He had been pinpoints of energy, nervous with the strain of his life, of being on the hook.

"Just be cool," Buddy had told him. "Once we're in the room, you can sleep until it's time to cut again."

But coming up the street they'd noticed nothing until they were almost to the basement door. Then they saw Mr. Pool up against the door. This man was chewing him out; Mr. Pool was taking it. When he saw Buddy and Junior, his eyes had been full of warning. Buddy and Junior walked briskly by. A teacher was holding open the door at the top of cement steps. She saw Junior and Buddy. They came on.

"We got to go in," Buddy had time to say.

"I can't," Junior said. But he kept the pace next to Buddy as they climbed the steps.

"We'll go into class and you let me do the

talking. Whatever happens, you wait for me to play it out," Buddy told Junior.

"Don't make me sit in no class," Junior said as they went inside.

In the school Junior and Buddy were attacked by noise. Noise fell over them as they climbed the staircase. The stairs were enclosed with a prison mesh from one floor to the next to keep students from accidentally falling over their open sides. Noise spilled out of the mesh and rose to an unbelievable pitch.

Junior was sweating.

"I think I remember," Buddy said. "We got one more floor to go. Man, I don't recall it being this bad."

The school was a modern, well-kept building but over-heated, holding body odors from day to day. Junior and Buddy had to climb through the smells and noise until they came to the right floor. They found their homeroom. They went in and took seats in the back. Some teacher, some woman they didn't know, stood behind the desk looking over her attendance book and checking off students' names. Every now and again she looked up. When she noticed Junior and Buddy, she hesitated in her checking and turned the pages back to sheets of previous months.

Buddy jumped up, moving fast through one of the aisles. He didn't know what he would do; he simply felt he ought to take command

and do something. Why should he let her discover that he and Junior were on the hook? Better that he give the information to her. Somehow there was pride in that.

"Hey, miss? Teacher, my friend can't find his science book. Please, would you have an extra he could use?"

The teacher eyed Buddy. She was a cool lady. She was black. There was warmth of humor deep down behind the dark of her eyes. However, she let the humor die away. Obviously she was as tough as Buddy, been around long enough to know all the games. Wise enough, she had come too far and had worked too hard trying to teach something to let one fast-talking kid put it over on her.

"What's your name?" she said.

"My friend back there is Junior Brown." Innocently, Buddy stared at her.

"I asked you your name," she said, her mouth tightening ever so slightly.

"I'm Buddy Clark."

"I've been here two months," she said, "and I haven't seen either one of you before. Take these passes to the office." She wrote out paper slips for each of them and handed them to Buddy.

"All we need is a science book," Buddy said. He let himself make this quiet plea but he would not stoop to beg.

The teacher said nothing in reply. She gave

him one hard, unsmiling look. Buddy knew he and Junior had had it. He got Junior up and out of the room with all the kids looking at them. Some kids giggled; some just looked at them blankly. Buddy couldn't remember the kids anymore. Slowly he recalled a few faces but they seemed different now. He had traveled so far from these kids in just a couple of months that they seemed tired and patient, like old folks, old people sitting in a clinic somewhere.

Hall monitors had taken positions on every floor of the building. Buddy and Junior had no chance to sneak away. Their passes were checked and they had to go on to the office. Inside, Buddy handed the passes to some secretary. She told Buddy and Junior to sit down and while they sat, she took the passes into another office.

Buddy couldn't believe how calm he was. Everything had happened so quickly, he hadn't had time to get himself scared. What could they do to him, anyway? He wasn't sure. He hadn't committed any crime, he didn't think. He had just been on the hook. Would they turn him over to Juvenile Court for that? He didn't know.

"I know one thing," he said quietly to Junior. "Nobody's going to make us stay in any class. And nobody's going to put us away in no reformatory."

Junior was scared. "What are they going to make us do?" he said. "I have to get out—Buddy, why can't we just go?"

Buddy knew if they walked out, providing nobody got in their way, it would be Junior who would get caught. Buddy could disappear, hiding in a hundred different places; they would never even know where to start looking. But not Junior. Junior had just one place to go and they could always find him.

Buddy had to laugh. Why was he pretending when he knew nobody cared whether he or Junior came or went?

If Mr. Pool hadn't got caught, we would be in the basement and nobody would never even miss us, Buddy thought. It's just when you get in their way once that they see you and have to do something.

"Listen," Buddy told Junior. "Some assistant principal is going to look over our records and probably tell us we have to go to class every day, or we'll be put on detention, if we haven't been already. And maybe when you've been on detention long enough they do something bad to you. Anyhow, they're going to say we got to go to class."

"What if they send a note to my mother?" Junior said.

"Look, haven't I taken care of the notes?" Buddy said. He had taken care to read and to destroy every note they gave Junior when he first went on the hook a few days at a time. Mr. Pool had taken care of all the office pink slips that went into the attendance officer's box.

"What if they call her on the phone?" Junior said.

That's the problem, Buddy thought. They could call up Junior's mother if one of the pink slips got past Mr. Pool. But they wouldn't because nobody cared about Junior. Nobody wanted him or even missed him. Buddy knew he couldn't tell Junior that.

"You just don't worry," Buddy said. "Let's wait and see what's going down."

They waited almost an hour before some man came out and motioned them to come with him. They went through the office to the back room where the man worked. He had chairs arranged for them in front of his desk.

The AP was a black dude with wavy, black hair. He wore a tweed sports coat. Both Junior and Buddy figured at the same time that he wasn't Puerto Rican or Haitian. He was Mr. Rountree, according to the name plate on his desk.

"I'm the assistant principal," he told them. Like they hadn't figured that one out yet. They could tell Mr. Rountree was feeling good about himself, about his suit, about where he was.

What do you do with a dude like that? Buddy wondered. What do you do when your hair won't even make an Afro?

Buddy was feeling mean. The whole business of school made him sick. Here was this Rountree cat who probably was a decent cat. But the dude had got himself tied up with working himself higher and higher so he could keep wearing those good-looking jackets.

No. Maybe he's all right. Maybe he believes he can help the kids by being with them when they find out how much they don't have.

Buddy gave up trying to figure out the dude. For a minute he didn't even feel like protecting Junior.

Buddy thought, Let Junior find out what it's all about. Time he knew what was going down.

"Which one of you is Junior Brown?" the dude said.

Junior waved his hand and shifted slightly in his seat. He was so used to being in the presence of authority, he knew how to act. He was calm.

"Then you're Buddy Clark," the dude said, turning to Buddy.

Now that's cool, Buddy thought. You're using your head.

"Yessir," Buddy said stiffly. He kept his voice gruff and thick.

The dude was looking at him, at the way he was dressed. Buddy had been in his windbreaker for days because the weather was so cold. There were dirt creases all over it. The wrists and collar were grimy.

As the dude flicked his eyes away from Buddy over to Junior, Buddy had a chance to think. Once, Doum Malach had told him, "Caution and camouflage." And as the dude studied Junior Brown's nice-looking sweater and high-priced shoes, Doum's words sounded inside Buddy.

The dude turned back to Buddy. By that time, Buddy already knew that the dude was going to try to psyche him.

The dude sure did have some cool eyes. Buddy was about to stare him down when "caution and camouflage" again clicked in his head.

Be the poor boy. Let him know you are tight with Junior but you ain't living off him. Show him you like Junior and want what Junior has. But then why are you on the hook? Why is Junior?

Buddy lowered his eyes, unable to sort out the posture he should take.

"Until two and a half months ago, you boys had a fairly good record," Rountree told them. "Obviously both of you are better equipped than most students."

Buddy kept his eyes down, for the dude was trying to psyche both of them.

"Then, for some reason, you both went on the hook. You deliberately blew everything. Now I want to know why."

Buddy figured this was their chance to confess and get themselves straight with the school. For a fleeting moment he thought how great it would be to see the dude's face when he told him about the hidden room in the basement, about the solar system and Mr. Pool.

Blow his mind!

Instead Buddy played the only game he knew might work. Camouflage.

Buddy looked deep into the palm of his hand and sighed. He raised his eyebrows in surrender, knowing the dude was watching his every move. Slowly he turned his head to glance at Junior Brown. Junior was looking at the dude, pleading. He was leaning forward, hanging on the dude's words.

Buddy stared at his hand again.

We sorry to miss school but you know, we had our troubles. We were too proud to ask for any help. We didn't want nobody to pity us.

"I'm giving you a chance," the dude told them. His voice was not unkind. "Can't either of you tell me what's been going on?"

There was a pause before Buddy blurted out: "We haven't done a thing wrong!" He allowed his voice to sound resentful and to stutter over the words. But he would say no more. Junior said nothing.

The dude shuffled his papers. This time, when he spoke, he was cold as ice.

"You boys have broken the Compulsory Education Law by being out of school while still minors. This institution can press charges against you and your parents. If we do press charges, both of you will be taken away from your parents and sent to reform school."

Junior had to hold onto the arms of his chair, his hands commenced to jump so. He turned to Buddy, stunned.

Buddy hadn't known how much fear he had deep within himself. Now the fear rose inside him, turning him numb. Buddy took hold of the fear and lay it out in front of him, like a deck of cards.

The dude picked up the telephone on his desk.

"Outside line," Rountree said into the phone. He looked at Buddy. "I have a number here for a Lucille Clark who is your aunt. Now I'm going to call her and get her down here, right now if I can. And then I'm calling Junior Brown's mother and I'm going to get her down here too."

Junior, how could you do this to me? Aren't you ashamed!

Junior's mother entered his thought and took it tightly in her hand. But before she could say another word to Junior, she began to cough and wheeze.

Junior staggered to his feet. Buddy started talking fast. Junior sat down, trembling, and sweating down his sides.

All his life Buddy had feared being somehow caught and locked up someplace where he couldn't get out. Desperately he took a single ace out of his fearful deck of cards. He played it.

"That's not my address anymore," Buddy said. "My aunt, she went back down to Texas so I had to move in with her brother who is my uncle, Mr. Malach."

"What's his number?" the dude said.

Buddy gave the dude the number. "He isn't home," Buddy said. "That's the number of his newsstand. He's got a phone and he's always there this time of day."

The dude dialed the number. Doum answered promptly.

Come on, Doum. You my friend, I know you are.

"Mr. Malach? Good morning to you, sir. I'm Mr. Rountree, the assistant principal at your nephew, Buddy Clark's school. Now he says he is living with you . . ."

Rountree paused. Buddy waited. Junior Brown kept his eyes on the black phone in Rountree's hand.

The dude picked up his pencil and wrote on a sheet in Buddy's folder.

". . . About five months?" the dude said into the phone. "Okay. Now, Mr. Malach, were you aware that for more than two months, your nephew hasn't been in school? He and his friend, Junior Brown, came back this morning.

That's right. I'm afraid being sorry isn't going to help. This is a serious matter, you know. We have a Compulsory Education Law and under it, you as well as your nephew can be prosecuted."

There was a long pause. The dude wrote on the sheet. "Harlem Hospital?" the dude said into the phone. "When were you released?" The dude wrote it down. "Now, you say both boys worked your newsstand while you were in the hospital?"

Doum must have given an elaborate explanation on the other end of the phone.

Buddy let himself relax inside. He allowed Doum to take care of everything. But he was ashamed of himself for never trusting Doum.

Here he is, saving my life, Buddy thought. I could have told Doum about the planets. He could've been my friend.

Just before the dude was ready to hang up, he asked Doum to come down to the school right away. Then the dude gave Doum the school phone number and his own extension. He hung up. They waited. A few minutes passed and the phone rang.

"Yes," the dude said. He waited while Doum talked on the other end. "But I really wanted to get this taken care of this afternoon," the dude said. (Pause) "Well, I don't want you to close it down. (Pause) I agree, they're worth it. They aren't ordinary kids out on the hook; they get good grades. (Pause) All right, then, I'll expect you here—it's on the fourth floor—the first thing in the morning. Just come in and tell the secretary you have an appointment with Mr. Rountree."

That was it. The dude hung up. He closed Buddy's file and opened Junior's.

Oh, no, Buddy thought.

Rountree picked up the phone.

"Let's see." The dude looked at Junior. "Your mother is Junella Brown."

Junior got to his feet again, his mouth hanging open.

"Sir," Buddy said, "please, don't call his mother."

The dude looked at Buddy. "So she doesn't know, either," the dude said.

"He was only helping me out with the newsstand," Buddy said. "His mother will kill herself."

"What are you trying to say?" the dude said.

Buddy took a calculated deep breath and then blurted out what he knew about Mrs. Brown's asthma, about the oxygen mask, about the needle and the epinephrine.

It all sounded plausible. "I mean," Buddy finished, "Junior is her only child. His daddy is away all week and so Junior and his mother are real close. If she knew he wasn't in school, she could just have an attack and Junior wouldn't be there. Nobody'd be there."

There was nothing the dude could do but put the phone down.

"It's a terrible situation with you boys," the dude said. "Here we have a sick mother of one of you and a sick uncle of the other. The problem isn't easy. If you had to work, you could have told the school. With your grades, you might have worked part-time starting about two o'clock in the afternoon." The dude stopped and looked very troubled. "We have these kinds of problems every day. A fourth of the students here have to work to help out their families. Do you think they all go on the hook? No, of course not. We arrange for them to work part-time. We're not their enemy— when are you going to learn that the school is all you've got? We want you here and getting an education!"

The dude was serious, that's what Buddy couldn't get over. Rountree really believed what he was telling them.

So you get an education, Buddy wanted to tell him. So what? Half of the educated cats on the street couldn't remember the last time they had even a lousy job.

"All right, Virgil Brown, I will give it to you straight as I can."

Buddy and Junior were both startled to hear the dude use Junior's given name.

"I'm going to trust you to tell your mother

to be here the first thing tomorrow morning
when school opens."

Tell the dude you'll tell her to be here. In
his mind Buddy prompted Junior.

Just lie! Tell him anything so we can get out
of here!

Junior couldn't say a word. He was huge and
silent, racked with tiny tremors.

The dude wrote out two more passes. When
he finished, he gave them to Buddy.

"This will get you into the Third Period
class. You'd better hurry because it's a half-
hour mode and you are about to miss it."

Buddy took the passes and he and Junior
got out of there as fast as they could.

They left Rountree sitting at his desk with
a sneaking suspicion gnawing at him. He
glanced at Junior's file again. After a long
moment he picked up the phone.

"Outside line," he said. When he had the
outside, he dialed Mrs. Junella Brown. He let
the phone ring but there was no answer. He
never did have any luck getting hold of
mothers of students in the morning. They were
always out shopping or doing laundry somewhere. He hung up and was at once confronted
with some student's aching-tired, irritated
mother with two small children hanging to her
coat.

"I figured I waited long enough so I come
on in," she said. "I got to get these kids to

Day-care. Going to be late for my job as it is. Mable Johnson," she told Rountree. "My sister took your message, say you wanted to see me. I wants to see *you*. What you all trying to say Ronnie done!"

Mr. Rountree had time enough to scoop up the folders of Junior Brown and Buddy Clark and shove them in his desk drawer before the five-foot, skinny, tough mother of Ronald Johnson cornered him behind his desk.

Junior and Buddy made it to their class just in time for the ringing of the buzzer. They handed the teacher their passes and retreated with the flow of students heading for other classrooms. They managed to reach the basement stairs on the first floor.

"We're taking us a chance," Buddy panted to Junior, "but I got to see about Mr. Pool."

At the foot of the stairs Buddy had to find a key to fit the heavy, inside door. It took him awhile, frantically searching through his keys to find a skeleton key that would fit. He did find one though, and, turning the key in the lock, he held his breath as the door swung open to his touch. Halfway down the corridor they stopped to listen, then went on cautiously to the broom closet. They went in, dropping their books in one dark corner. They moved one wall back and entered the hidden room. All was dark. Mr. Pool wasn't there. Suddenly they could hear voices in the corridor. They waited, not moving a muscle. Footsteps. No, kids above them. A sound, claw-like, a muffled rattling, slowly quieted. It was close to noon before Mr. Pool could chance coming to the basement room. When he did come, he tiptoed in.

"Buddy? Junior?"

"We're here," Buddy said, whispering. "Where you been? What's happening? I got to talk to you."

"Did you get caught?" Mr. Pool asked them. He skirted the darkened planets—gently touching them as he headed toward the sound of Buddy.

"They caught us," Buddy told him. "They going to have Junior tell his mother to come down here tomorrow morning, but you know he can't. I'm supposed to bring this cat I work for, who I'm supposed to be living with and who's supposed to be my uncle. Only I don't live with him and he ain't my uncle."

"I got caught too," Mr. Pool said.

"We saw it happen," Buddy told him. "What all the man say to you?"

"Nothing he can prove," Mr. Pool told him. "Just say he can never find me, which is a fact. But I do my work. I do my job. Trouble is, they want me to do the whole job and when they say to do it."

Junior listened to Mr. Pool. Comfortable in the dark, he felt warm.

"All right now," Mr. Pool said. He turned on the juice of the solar system so they could have some light. At once the room was transformed, for Junior especially, into deep space and glowing, revolving spheres.

"Oh, that's so pretty," Junior said. "It's the first time I been here when you turn it on."

"Yes, it's pretty," Mr. Pool said. "Ain't it so, Buddy?"

"Yea," Buddy said, "but I'm worried for it."

They knew what he meant.

"Look at the planet of Junior Brown," Mr. Pool told them.

They looked at the great planet. It was brown. It was stupendous. Somehow the other planets were mere copies of spheres already known. The planet of Junior Brown had come to life right in the room, out of themselves and how they felt about one another.

"Listen," Mr. Pool said. "I got to dismantle the whole thing." His bald head glistened. Its shining, anxious heat was the signal telling Junior and Buddy that the end was near.

"In other words," Mr. Pool said, "we got to vacate the premises." He spoke glibly, trying to make it easy on the boys. But Mr. Pool had no idea where he could rebuild the solar system. And he feared for Junior and Buddy if they stayed on the hook and took to the streets.

"Junior Brown is fixin' ta die," Junior said.

In his folding chair he spoke as a sage. He was Buddha tamping the eternal light.

"Don't put my sun out yet," Buddy told him.

Mr. Pool said, "I'll have to start taking everything apart tonight and be finished with it by tomorrow night. I don't know what to do with it." He lifted his hands, but kept them from touching the spheres. "I guess I can pack up everything and take it home. I bet I could get it all in a good-sized foot locker or cardboard box."

Mr. Pool felt suddenly foolish. Here he was acting like a child, building himself some forbidden toy and playing with it in secret. He'd best be thinking about keeping his job. The thought of his job made him angry. What had come over him anyhow? No job or the hidden room, either, was more important than the one thing he knew to be true.

"The human race is bound to come one time," he said, through the whirl of planets. He never was sure what he meant by always having to say that. But to his soul he knew Junior and Buddy were forerunners on the road down which the race would have to pass.

In the dimness Buddy blinked. Then his eyes widened and shone back the light in a stunning thought.

"Maybe it's already come," he said. "Maybe the race is been here and is still here and you don't know where to find it."

Mr. Pool had to smile. "If I don't know, then who does?" he said.

In the folding chair Junior rocked and rocked. "Say I got to tell my mother to come on down here," Junior said. "Say I'll go to reform school if I don't."

"He talking about Mr. Rountree," Buddy told Mr. Pool. "Tomorrow morning that old AP going to catch up to all the lies we told him."

Mr. Pool looked sympathetically from Buddy to Junior. "You boys got real unlucky," he said. "It's a darn shame!" Grimly he smiled. "Rountree will have to get the attendance officer on you, or maybe worse, when you don't show up. But where for you to go, there's the worry." Mr. Pool rubbed his forehead as though to wipe it of pain.

They all fell silent. Only Buddy had continued thinking clearly. "This is the last time we can come here," he said.

"I don't see why," Mr. Pool said. "You been coming here. You got caught one time but it don't mean you'll be caught again. I won't be caught again, either."

"What if Rountree is out there waiting for us in the morning?" Buddy said.

Mr. Pool told him, "Rountree will wait in his office like he's supposed to. Don't you worry, just come here a little earlier, if you want."

Tomorrow was Friday. Buddy remembered, he had to go with Junior to Miss Peebs' house on Friday. He looked at Mr. Pool. "You say you will be here tomorrow night?"

"I'll have everything put away by then," Mr. Pool said.

Buddy turned to Junior. "What you going to do about tomorrow?" he said to Junior. "How you going to tell your mother to be here?"

But Junior wouldn't say. He sat there, rocking, watching the solar system come to an end. Buddy dropped to the floor; with his arms hugging his knees, he watched Mr. Pool. Tediously they all waited out the day for school to be over. Only after the last buzzer sounded and all the teachers had gone did Buddy and Junior prepare to leave.

"I'm counting on you," Mr. Pool thought to tell Buddy at the door. "It's not fair of me, I know, but I depend on you."

With tiredness showing in his eyes, Buddy looked fondly on Mr. Pool. If he could have a father, he would have only this man. "I got a feeling," Buddy said, "everything's going to be all right."

The two of them made their escape. Buddy accompanied Junior all the way to Junior's house. On the steps outside he told Junior, "I'll pick you up early tomorrow." They stood there with Junior answering nothing.

Buddy would have liked to have known what Junior would tell his mother but he wouldn't ask Junior again. He left. He turned on his heel and let Junior go up alone.

Junior entered his mother's apartment. His mother was there for him, as she always was. She was here but this time she didn't rush to meet him. She didn't pick at him or question him with her bright watching. His mother acted distant, strange. She retreated to the kitchen while he put his outer garments away. Junior wondered about her silence only for a moment. He was worn out. He went to his room, unwilling to face her without knowing what he would say. Junior found his room neat and clean, as usual. He went straight to the bed and fell heavily across it.

"What am I going to do?" Junior wondered. He closed his eyes but he couldn't sleep. Exhausted, his mind tumbled with thinking. He felt almost glad to be nearly finished with hiding in the basement room. Months of sitting in the dark hiding place had become monotonous. Days of sitting had bored him close to death. Only with Mr. Pool and Buddy's construction of the solar system had his mind been occupied for a while.

Junior is fixin ta die. If I tell Mama to come to school, then what? Friday, I got to go see Miss Peebs. Saturday, Daddy comes home. Sometimes. Then what?

Junior thought and thought. With his eyes closed, all was night. He could be red.

Junior jumped, remembering something. He slid to the edge of the bed and looked underneath it. In a moment he let the bedspread fall back over the box spring. Grunting, he hurled himself over to the closet.

I was sleepy this morning. I could have put the canvas away.

Junior knew he hadn't taken The Red Man up. Inside his closet, he found his paint box and the piece of wood he used for mixing paints, but no Red Man. Suddenly Junior felt too heavy to stand up any longer. He lurched for the bed and lay there panting until he had calmed. At suppertime his mother called him. She wouldn't come into his room to get him.

Junior ate his supper alone in the kitchen. He ate slowly everything she had placed on the table for him to eat. His mother had disappeared in her own room, closing the door firmly behind her.

No use his looking for The Red Man. His mother would have got rid of it by now. Cutting it to pieces, she would have burned The Red Man piece by painted piece in the kitchen sink.

No use for him ever to explain to her. Seeing all those people living in The Red Man— doing awful things, she would say—his mother knew now that she hadn't known him at all.

The Red Man people just had been living their lives. With that thought Junior knew what he had to do. So he ate his food, savoring its rich taste, loving it tightly, the way some folks love a gamble.

Junella Brown sat in her rocker next to the big bed in her bedroom. She had her arms crossed tightly below her narrow chest. Her legs were crossed one over the other just as tightly, and her eyes were fixed on the closed door.

She had found the canvas with the paint still wet, under Junior's bed, when she had entered his room to clean it this very morning. As she was making his bed, her foot knocked against the edge of something. Stooping down to see, she'd pulled out that big canvas Junior had been painting. At first Junella couldn't tell what it was but something made her go search Junior's desk for his magnifying glass. When she found the glass, she came back; she got on her knees to examine the painting.

"Oh, what an awful thing!" she whispered now. "What a terrible, sick thing he's done!"

Junella watched the door. If Junior came to the room, she would have to face him. She hoped he wouldn't. She wanted to wait for his father to come home.

The painting had been full of people involved with one another in a way Junella knew

any decent boy would never think to draw.
And to see how he had squeezed them all in
this red, red figure of a man! Is that what
Junior's mind was full of? Images of people
living their most private lives? And Junior had
painted whole streets of people—robbers,
drunkards—people hurting one another. There
had even been a figure that resembed herself.
There had been that boy, that Buddy Clark,
who was everywhere in the painting, all over
the streets.

If there was some way she could get that
Buddy Clark sent away, Junella could then
maybe help Junior back to reality.

Junior had been in the painting, like a single
brown ball bouncing on street corners, jiving
in school yards. Junior had painted himself
everywhere in the city where he had no business being!

Junella had experienced a mild asthma attack after finding the painting. She had needed
to use the nebulizer but had come out of the
attack only slightly weakened. Afterward she'd
slept for some time. When she awoke, she'd
returned to Junior's room and taken care of
that painting. Wet as it was, she didn't dare
burn it, so she sent it down the incinerator
with the rest of her garbage.

"That's that," she said from the rocker. "I'll
never give him canvas again as long as I live."

After he'd eaten his supper, Junior went back to his room and played the piano half-heartedly. He didn't emerge from his room until morning. Only once did Junella come out of her bedroom, to clean up the kitchen after Junior and to wash up in the bathroom. Then she went directly to her room. She stayed there, controlling herself so she would not bring on another attack. In the morning she rose with the alarm clock ringing and at once went in to prepare Junior's breakfast. She would not say a word to him, she told herself. He would have to come to her and ask her for help.

Junella prepared Junior a good, hearty meal, just the kind he liked. She was certain that with the breakfast they could sit down and have a good conversation about what he had done.

"I destroyed that painting, Junior, because I know you weren't yourself when you thought to paint it." Yes, that was the kind of thing she might say to him when they sat down to talk.

Standing in the dining room, she called Junior to come for breakfast. Then Junella went back to the kitchen and sat down. *"You can never have materials for painting, Junior, until you can demonstrate to me you will occupy your mind with thoughts proper and normal for your age group."* Yes, she could say that. Junior had always been the kind of boy who was obedient, who listened to his parents.

When his father gets here, the two of them can talk man to man, Junella thought. Oh, thank God for a man like Walter for the boy. He would know just what to say to bring Junior back to right thinking.

Junior was slow coming to breakfast this morning. When Junella knocked on his bedroom door, there was no answer. She looked in. Junior wasn't there.

Junior had fled the house long before Junella's alarm went off. He had taken his paint box, his music and that funny, childish wind-up toy he always kept on his desk. He'd even taken his raincoat, his best shoes and new brown cashmere sweater. He'd worn his best suit.

If Junella had thought quickly enough, she would have realized that Junior took mostly that which would keep him warmest on cold winter nights. She thought only that Junior was angry over the painting. She figured he would stay out late with that Buddy Clark of his, way late, past his lesson and maybe past his bedtime.

"All right then," she told herself. "You can just stay out there, but you'll get hungry. You'll get cold and tired and then you'll head for home. Oh, it's a lesson some boys have to learn. I won't get myself sick over it. You wait until your father gets home!"

Mr. Pool had taken it upon himself to care for them this day. Junior and Buddy. In the basement room Mr. Pool had brought enough supplies to last them a good five days. With the way Junior Brown could eat, maybe no more than three days, Buddy thought. Still there was lots of stuff. There was a good-sized carton with two thermos bottles of hot chocolate. There were hard-boiled eggs, a half gallon of milk and lots of sweet rolls wrapped in plastic wrap to keep them fresh. There were egg salad sandwiches, ham sandwiches and cheese sandwiches. There was even a jar of pickles and a half-pack of cold beer for Mr. Pool.

"Man-o-man!" Buddy said, "we going to have ourselves a party!"

"Help yourselves," Mr. Pool said. "You can't walk out of here until everybody else is long gone."

Junior dropped his suitcase on the floor, flung off his raincoat and sweater and attacked the food. Buddy was hungry too, but what he wanted most was something hot to drink. He was beginning to believe that cold, like inches, was a part of his growing. He had even said so earlier to Doum Malach. Old Doum had told him this story. "We are deeply opposed to cold," Doum had told him. "That's why the white folks turn it on us about every six months."

Remembering, Buddy had to smile. Doum was crazy but his was a good kind of crazy that tried to protect you. He hadn't even mentioned to Buddy the fact that Buddy had used him in a lie to Mr. Rountree.

For a moment Buddy thought fondly of Doum. Then, eagerly, he took up a thermos and found the chocolate steaming. It burned his mouth but he gulped it down all the same, as though he'd never tasted anything quite like it.

"Oh, man," Buddy said, "that's precious stuff." He wiped his mouth. With the thermos in hand, he turned to Junior. Junior had all but eaten one ham sandwich and had started on a hard-boiled egg. Junior had taken the other thermos of chocolate.

"Wait up for me," Buddy told him. "You going to eat it all before I get to sit down good."

"Shuh," Junior said, not unkindly. Junior couldn't be too unkind even to Buddy when he was eating.

Chewing on a sandwich, Buddy thought to ask Mr. Pool, "How come you brought so much stuff?"

Mr. Pool was busy with a long rectangle of a box about a foot square and maybe five feet long. He had stuffed the bottom of the box with crumpled newspaper. Now he gently shoved the sun in. Their solar system was in the process of coming down. Mr. Pool had attached a forty-watt bulb on a cord to Junior's chair to give himself enough light to work by.

Without knowing it they had all braced themselves for this coming apart of worlds. Now Buddy and Junior could see it happening and not lose heart. The food was a big help, a comfort. Mr. Pool had known it would be.

"I figured I'd bring enough to eat for today, of course," Mr. Pool said, "and maybe have some left over for tomorrow. But from the looks of things I'm going to have to start over buying the first thing Saturday morning."

"You mean for us to stay here?" Buddy asked him.

"I don't know even yet," Mr. Pool told him. "I'm packing up everything, though. I'll have this box filled tonight. After that, I don't know. We'll be ready to stay or ready to go."

"Go, more better than likely," Buddy said.

"But where?" Mr. Pool asked him.

"I got the whole day to worry over it," Buddy said. He glanced at Junior. Still eating, Junior hadn't told Buddy one thing about what he was planning to do. He had come out of his house way early this morning all dressed up and with that suitcase banging his leg. Buddy hadn't bothered to ask Junior what was

in the case. It was Friday. Junior had nothing
else in his hands. He knew Junior's Fake Book,
at least, was inside the suitcase. And Junior
must have taken whatever else a body would
think to want when they were running from
home. Junior was wearing those sharp clothes
of his all at the same time.

"You going to burn up in all that," Buddy
had told him, knowing how Junior couldn't
stand to wear so much clothing.

"Give you my sweater to wear," Junior had
told him, "maybe even my raincoat. But first,
let's get us on out of here."

They'd gone quickly in the morning light;
the cold sun had been behind them, eyeing
them without heat. Even then, Buddy hadn't
asked Junior if he'd told his mother about
coming to school.

That's why Junior cut out early, Buddy
thought. Junior didn't tell her and he ain't
going to be around when she finds out.

Mr. Pool spent a good while packing and un-
packing one or two plastic planets to see how
he could arrange them to fit in the box in the
least amount of space.

"You shouldn't put them in first," Buddy
told him.

"I know that, son," Pool said, "I just am
figuring. The tracks have got to be straightened
and put in first. Then the rods and cords, but

that's going to take me more time than I can give this here morning."

Mr. Pool had to go out and see to the school.

"You want the light on?" Buddy asked Junior after Mr. Pool had gone. With the light on there was no way for them to avoid looking at the broken-down system.

"No," Junior said.

Buddy turned off the light bulb. Leaping darkness closed in on them. Junior was full and comfortable in the dark. He felt warm but not hot. He bunched up his raincoat for a pillow and stretched out on the floor. "Buddy?"

"Yea," Buddy said.

"Come take my sweater."

"Oh, man!" Buddy said. He removed his jacket and fumbled through the dark for Junior's sweater. When he had hold of it, he just felt it for a minute. It felt like the softest wool in the world. Buddy eased himself into it.

"I hate to rub up on this floor with it," Buddy said. He thought to spread out his jacket. Then, he placed himself carefully on the jacket so that Junior's sweater never touched the floor.

So it was that the day passed for Buddy and Junior. They slept a while there on the floor. They awoke, they ate again and later they talked quietly with Mr. Pool. No one found them out.

7

Junior," Buddy whispered, "what is going on?" "Shhhh!" It was Miss Peebs.

The moment Buddy walked inside Miss Peebs' house, he knew all his years in the street hadn't prepared him for such a place.

On all sides in this great, long hallway were mountains of shrouded things. White, giant monsters pressed in on Buddy in the dim, mad place, as he walked a narrow tightrope of a path. He brought up the rear. Junior was in front of him. The crazy woman led the way.

Buddy thought of turning around and just going to the foyer and out the front door. He dared not look behind him. There were those dead, giant things even in back of him. He felt the hair all over him tickle and seem to rise.

You could die here. Some big things would come out from behind the dead giants and

carve a hole in you. Or she might do it when
you had your mind on those giants coming to
life.

The moment she opened the door, Buddy
knew Miss Peebs was crazy. He had taken one
look at the silk, all-black get-up she wore, her
pits of burning eyes, and he knew her mind
was lost behind the deadly yellow of her face.

With no light, the shrouded place of the
giants was creepy and shaded gray. Miss Peebs
had covered the piles of furniture in the hall
with muslin dust covers. Buddy kept his hands
taut at his sides. He didn't look left or right
but braced his body for any attack. Buddy
had only his nerve to fight with; he knew it
would never do.

Miss Peebs opened a door off the hallway.
They went in to a living room where there was
a ceiling light burning. Noise came screaming
at them from raised windows. Noise knocked
into tier upon tier of piled things—chests and
bureaus, chairs and bookcases.

Dust choked Buddy and noise bit at the
dust settling on his skin. The only silence anywhere was a comfortable sofa with soft pillows.
There was a monster but it had no shroud.
It was a great dark roundness with teeth and
black, shredded gums.

Actually, Miss Peebs' piano was a pool of
beauty. Buddy had been so ready for giants,

he hadn't seen it for what it was. It was just a long and lovely piano. It was a perfect thing in the room.

Buddy stared around with his mouth open at the piles and piles of stuff with no space for questions or even answers. His eyes paused at something by the windows. It was the one place in the room that was covered by a white shroud. Square and flat under its coverlet, it was a separate, gleaming patch of white amidst chaos, like moonlight on a battlefield.

Buddy walked over to the couch and sat stiff and straight on the edge of it. Junior was standing on the path just beyond the couch, with Buddy on one side and the piano on the other. Miss Peebs was in front of him, standing sideways on the path.

Junior had been so relieved to find Miss Peebs' piano in one piece. But then, he'd noticed the same shrouded place Buddy had seen. Fear rose in him. Wave upon wave of fear for the piano's safety made him shudder. The white, shrouded patch was like a bed, like a pen, to keep something confined.

"He's here," Miss Peebs said to Junior.

"I know," Junior said, "I can feel him."

He was shaking. His bulk seemed to sag at the knees. He was sweating all over his arms and back.

"Junior, I've got to get around you and to the piano," Miss Peebs said.

Junior stepped aside. Miss Peebs slid by him and sat down at the piano. At once, she began playing an atonal music.

"He knows you're here but you've got to see," she said. She looked at Junior and then at Buddy.

Buddy saw terror in Miss Peebs' eyes. Energy surrounded her like a magnetic field. Every molecule, every pore of her, was jiggling a hundred times too fast. He'd never seen anything like the power that came from her. And seeing her sheer strength, Buddy believed Miss Peebs could pick up that piano and throw it at him, if she'd wanted to.

What's going on? he thought. What do they want?

Junior was creeping along the main path of the room, away from the piano and couch.

Buddy thought, He's going to close the windows so the noise won't be so loud.

With the music Miss Peebs played all around him, the noise from outside seemed even louder to Buddy. A moment more of so much sound and he knew he would have to cover his ears.

Junior stopped on the path directly in front of that patch of white, like a hospital bed with nothing at all in it but cleanliness.

The piano was still. "You will do it." It was Miss Peebs.

Junior leaned over close to the patch and lifted the cover. The movement was like someone peeling back gauze to expose a wound.

Buddy couldn't see what Junior was doing but he saw the coverlet move; he knew the moment Junior peered inside. Instantly Junior's arms swept upward and out, like wings hit by sudden wind.

Buddy saw Junior leap back, as though something had hurled him away. Junior fell against a precarious hill of furniture at the side of the path. The furniture crashed to the floor. Off balance, Junior landed on top of some of it, with some of it thudding down on him.

Buddy jumped up and was pulling drawers and tables off Junior without even thinking. He flung the mess aside. A whole lot of rings rolled around on the floor. Buddy counted about six topless jars of Vicks salve where they had fallen.

Miss Peebs was behind Buddy. She reached for a Vicks jar. Unmindful that the salve was crusted with time and dust, she dug in for a finger full and swallowed the mess neatly in a single gulp. Again she dug her finger in and coated her neck with it. All this done in an absent-minded motion.

"Are you sick or something?" Buddy heard himself saying to her. Vicks vapor burned hot, then cold through his nostrils. He was so calm, he had not even paused in his urge to get Junior out from under the fallen furniture.

"You're full of dust," he said to Junior. He pulled Junior to his feet and then brushed Junior's clothing off as best he could.

"What's going on—this is crazy," Buddy said. Junior was holding on to him. He had one arm tightly around Buddy's neck. The other, he wrapped around Buddy's arm in a grip like a vise.

"Man?" Buddy said. Buddy saw that Junior had the terror, the energy, too. "Man?" he repeated.

Junior couldn't say anything. It was Miss Peebs who spoke from behind Buddy.

"It's that Junior has seen him. We both have seen him," she said.

Buddy pried Junior's hand from his arm, one finger at a time. With both arms free, he worked at getting Junior's arm from around his neck. He hadn't noticed until now but the pressure on his throat was unbearable. Buddy knocked his fist into Junior's armpit with most of his force. Only then did Junior relax his hold long enough for Buddy to break free.

"God Almighty!" Buddy said. Junior came toward him again. This time Buddy was ready for him. He shoved Junior back toward Miss Peebs before Junior could reach him.

Junior and Miss Peebs stood like they were

frozen there on the path, with Miss Peebs leaning around Junior to see and Junior with his head thrown back, his hands poised in midair.

Buddy turned around toward the windows. He studied that square patch of white that had so terrified Junior. He stepped over some furniture—rugs wrapped around a wood screen of some kind—and was lifting and folding back the white coverlet in one motion.

Buddy stood absolutely still. He was a statue made from ebony, his head down below his shoulders, with his hands holding the coverlet up and away from where he was looking. Buddy moved his head just enough to look back toward Junior and Miss Peebs.

They stared at Buddy with awful pleading and fear in their eyes. Yet their faces burned at him with relief at having him know at last.

"I have kept this to myself for so long," Miss Peebs said.

When Buddy spoke, his voice came from deep within his stillness. "I understand," he said.

"I just wanted you to see him," Junior said.

"It'll be all right," Buddy told him.

"Because I got to take him out of here right now," Junior said. "So you go on out and wait for me while I get him out. I just want you to be there in case I need you."

Miss Peebs: "Oh, Junior, would you do that for me? No, you can't do it. He's sick, he won't go."

"No, Junior," Buddy said, but neither Junior nor Miss Peebs was listening to him.

"He'll go," Junior told Miss Peebs. "He's been fooling with you, he ain't that sick. I can take him."

"No, Junior," Buddy said. "Oh, man, don't."

"You go on out and wait in the hall," Junior told him. Junior was afraid but he was smiling. It had come to him quite suddenly what he could do to save Miss Peebs and the grand piano too.

"You just stand out there, look at the elevator," Junior told Buddy. "You done seen him once so you just don't look at him anymore when I bring him out."

Buddy let his breath out in a ragged sigh. The stillness he had become fell to pieces and he began to tremble. He let the white coverlet drop over the patch and walked swiftly away, passing Junior and Miss Peebs, knocking over furniture as he went. Buddy moved boldly through the hallway of white, shrouded giants and out of the apartment.

Buddy stood knocking his head against the elevator door, making soft thuds which he didn't feel. He pressed his hands hard against the stippled wall on either side of the door, scraping his nails, just as hard, along the texture. This was the only way he could wait for Junior and keep himself from thinking.

When Junior came out of the apartment about five minutes later, Buddy immediately pressed the elevator button. He felt his spine tingle as Junior came up close behind him. Buddy knew Junior had the thing right with him. And when the elevator came, he stepped to one side. He turned away, keeping his head down, so that Junior and the thing Junior had with him could go in first.

Buddy entered the elevator and turned quickly around, facing the closing door. All the way down he rode with his head knocking against the door and with his arms outstretched as far as they would go on each side. No one would get on the elevator with them, with big Buddy staring out, blocking the entrance, with the monstrous fat boy grinning from the rear.

Outside, Buddy stayed in front of Junior and the thing with him. The night was evening dark, cold and clear, with a moon rising but seeming to Buddy like it was taking a slow roll down the topmost height of the Natural History Museum.

Buddy paused at the corner of Amsterdam and 78th Street and looked both ways along the avenue. He was trembling now, from cold and from fear. He still wasn't sure what Junior meant to do; he wasn't thinking clearly at all.

"You aren't going home," Buddy said to Junior behind him.

"I can't," Junior said. He was closer to Buddy than Buddy had imagined. "Can't take him home because Mama wouldn't have him in her house, he's so filthy. Can't go home anyway —by now, she know I ain't been to school."

Buddy shook his head rapidly and blinked the winter out of his eyes. Steam rose white and hissing from around a manhole cover in the street. A taxi rolled over the cover, making a large, echoing sound all of a sudden. Amsterdam was nearly empty in this after-supper night. Almost empty, it was time for the city of darkness to roll over the evening.

"With filthy socks," Buddy said, speaking about the thing traveling with Junior.

"You right," Junior said, up close to Buddy's ear, "and with busted-up shoes."

There was only one place left for them to go.

"I got the bus fare," Buddy told him. They went to the bus stop. When the bus came, they rode uptown without speaking. Buddy sat in a seat in front of Junior. He turned himself sideways toward the window. He could see outside but he couldn't see Junior. He could hear Junior talking to this thing with him. No longer afraid, Junior was telling the thing to stay quiet, that it would be over soon.

With Buddy sitting sideways, it appeared

that Junior was talking to him. Buddy said
nothing. As when helping someone hurt in the
street, he felt nothing. But he wanted to cry,
so he closed his eyes and hunched himself
tightly in his seat.

They rode with Junior talking. When they
were uptown, they walked off the bus and to
the school with Junior still talking. Going
ahead, Buddy unlocked the door of the basement, letting the door stand open as he walked
a short way down the pitch-black hall. Buddy
heard Junior coming with his terrible talking
and then the door closing. When Buddy knew
Junior was right behind him, he lit a match
and led the way. They made the broom closet
and the hidden room. They found Mr. Pool
like he'd always been.

"Say now!" Mr. Pool said, in greeting. "You
boys about to be hungry?"

The single, forty-watt bulb glowed in the
room. Mr. Pool had set up a card table in the
center where the solar system had been. On
the table were paper plates and plastic forks.
To the side of the plates were pint and quart
cartons of still warm Chinese food.

Gone were the spherical tracks of the solar
system once attached to the ceiling. Mr. Pool
had forced them into perpendiculars so they
would fit into his long box. Gone were the rods
from which the planets had been suspended,

having been fitted into the box, also. Only a few planets were left on the floor. Among them was the planet of Junior Brown. Mr. Pool meant to put Junior Brown away at the very last.

"It's all gone," Buddy said, staring at the ceiling. "Every bit and piece of it is all apart." Buddy's voice seemed to slide out of him, aching all the way. He began shaking violently. Mr. Pool came quickly and took him by the arm before he collapsed.

"You'd better sit down," Mr. Pool said, leading Buddy toward the one folding chair.

Junior already occupied the chair. That is, when he came in and saw all the Chinese food, he had taken up a quart and pint and had gone over to the chair. He didn't sit on the chair, but sat himself down on the floor in front of it, facing it. He ate and he talked very softly, rocking ever so smoothly back and forth. He seemed happy.

Seeing Junior like that and feeling the frightful tremors from Buddy's arm run through his own hand, Mr. Pool knew something awful had taken place.

"Tell me quick what happened," Mr. Pool said to Buddy.

"Oh, I don't know. I don't know," Buddy said. "It's all so crazy."

"You better tell me," Mr. Pool said. "Just

take your time. Here, sit on the box. I'll sit beside you. No, it might break. Here, sit down beside me on the floor."

They sat to one side of the table, where they could see the back of Junior Brown and the chair at the same time.

Once Buddy started talking, he found he couldn't stop himself. He went on and on about himself and Junior, about how they were always together and yet still far apart. He told Mr. Pool about the river and how Junior loved it. He told about Junior's father and Junior's house. He spoke about Junior's piano and Junior's mother and then he told about Miss Peebs and her relative.

"I seen how Junior's been scared," Buddy said, "since months ago. But he got more and more scared and he wouldn't talk why until he was about to burst with something he couldn't let himself say. I still don't get what all of it was," Buddy said. "Until the time Junior came on with Miss Peebs' relative and how I had to help him help her."

Buddy laughed, like a cry. His eyes welled and then the bright, wet tears flowed back inside him again. "He say this relative have a real bad disease," Buddy said. "He say how the relative is sick and dirty and stinking with filthy socks. Only then he says it's a lie, he never even seen the relative. I should of known right then. I should of figured it but I didn't."

"I think I understand now," Mr. Pool said. "You don't need to talk about it."

"No," Buddy said, "wait, let me tell you what went on."

Across from them Junior picked up the light bulb on its cord. He held the light, talking, whispering, as if he were explaining about it. Next he put the light down between the chair and himself. Junior stretched out on his side with his hands one over the other under his cheek, just like a child. From where Buddy sat, he was a mountain. With the bulb burning in front of him, Junior was a mountain with the summer sun coming up red behind it.

"You know how some birds will steal from the other's nest," Buddy said, "and how the other, when he finds his eggs is stolen, will go out and pick up something, anything he can find to take the place of what's been taken? One for one. One egg gone, the bird will pick up a button and put it in the nest. Two eggs gone, the bird will find a penny and put it in the nest. He'll sit on that button and that penny just like he will his eggs. And if the eggs hatch and the babies fly off, he'll still sit there on the button and the penny just forever if he has to. Forever."

Buddy ran his hand through his hair. Mr. Pool patted him gently on the shoulder. "You take it easy," Mr. Poll told him. "You don't have to talk anymore."

Buddy went on. "Her house was a nest," Buddy said. "That Miss Peebs' house with all those rooms was one big nest full of every stinking thing under the sun. I never knew a woman could hurt so bad. See, she just kept on piling in more and more stuff each time she lost. I never knew a woman could lose so many times.

"But she had this place in her living room," Buddy said. "I can't describe it. It was square and covered up; she and Junior were about to die over it. I mean, he had to go see what was in there; he had to. And when he did see, he just fell apart. It was the relative there, see, all covered up. This relative so dirty and filthy Miss Peebs had to get rid of him. Junior had to get rid of him, too, in order to get to play the piano."

Buddy stopped. He clenched his hands tight together, pressing them against the floor.

"So I go and look into this covered place," Buddy said. "There wasn't a thing there. The place was empty of everything except maybe for dust. There never had been anyone under there. The dirty, filthy relative was just what Junior saw and I guess what Miss Peebs saw. So," Buddy said.

"So," Mr. Pool said, "you brought him here."

"Not just Junior," Buddy said.

"I know. I mean, you brought the relative

here," Mr. Pool said. "Junior brought him in order to help his teacher."

"You know!" Buddy said.

Mr. Pool looked over to where Junior still rested contentedly on the floor.

"Yes, I know," Mr. Pool said.

Buddy let his head drop heavily to his chest as a feeling of relief spread through him.

"We'll have to get him to a hospital," Mr. Pool said. "I guess we'll have to call his mother. She'll be worried, he should have been home by now."

Mr. Pool seemed to be thinking out loud. Buddy stared at him.

"Something will have to be done for Miss Peebs," Mr. Pool went on. "Maybe Junior's mother can help her. And I'll have to let the school know about Junior . . ."

". . . You want to put him in a hospital?" Buddy broke in on Mr. Pool. He got to his feet, backing away. "I been seeing people like Junior all the time," Buddy said. "Nobody bothers about 'em. But you put Junior in a hospital and he won't never come out. They'll lose him in one of those wards!"

"Buddy," Mr. Pool said, "son, listen!"

"No!" The tears Buddy had held back for so long filled his eyes. He felt betrayed and choking, he wouldn't let Mr. Pool touch him. "They'll hit on how fat he is," Buddy cried, "they'll say that's it, we got to get him skinny."

"Buddy, Buddy," Mr. Pool said.

"They'll see how black he is," Buddy said, "and they'll say that's the problem, we got to get to the white inside. How could you do that to him! You ain't going to take him to no hospital—I'll fight you, man, I'm telling you!"

Mr. Pool grabbed Buddy by the shoulders, shaking him. For a moment the two of them scuffled, struggling against one another. Finally Mr. Pool was able to shove Buddy against the wall. The effort took all of his strength.

"You're going to listen to me," Mr. Pool told Buddy. "Now listen! I'm not trying to hurt Junior. I wouldn't hurt him. All I mean is, he's got to have professional help. You know he is. You've seen people talking to themselves, stopping in the street or standing in the subway."

"And do they hurt anyone?" Buddy said. "No, man! They don't hurt *nobody*."

"They hurt themselves," Mr. Pool told him. "Don't you understand? Junior sees this person, this man, and that's serious. No," Mr. Pool said. "We have to get him some help but maybe first we can buy him some time."

"Time?" Buddy said. He looked anxiously at Mr. Pool.

"He might still need a hospital," Mr. Pool said, "but maybe not right away. Because putting him in there right away would be like telling him nobody cares about him. He has

to have time to know there's people who care.
We care. We want to see he gets well."

"Then what do we do?" Buddy said.

"Maybe we can find him a place for a
while," Mr. Pool said. "Some place close by so
we can look out for him. He needs time and he
needs us. I can put the school off and I think
I can take care of his parents, too."

"That's it!" Buddy said. He wiped his wet
face on his sleeve. "We got to hide him. By
Saturday, his daddy's going to be looking for
him—" Suddenly Buddy's eyes shone in as-
tonishment as that vague, stunning idea of what
to do with Junior caught up with him again.

Buddy smiled. "Maybe not," he said. "I
figure his daddy won't make it home this week
either."

"Time," Mr. Pool said. "Junior needs just
that much of a break for himself."

On the other side of the room, Junior was
standing up, backing away from the chair and
talking a mile a minute in fear, now, of the
thing with him.

"You stay down, you hear? Stay down. Stay
there!" Junior's voice was oddly expressionless.
Mr. Pool went over to him to calm him down.
He gave Junior a tall glass of milk.

"He won't stay down," Junior told Mr. Pool.

"Then let him walk around," Mr. Pool said.

"He going to try to bolt," Junior told Mr.
Pool.

"He can't get out, the door is locked," Mr. Pool said. He saw by the movement of Junior's frightened eyes that the thing was walking around the room.

"I'm tired," Junior said.

"Yes, sit down awhile and rest yourself," Mr. Pool said. "Sit down in the chair."

Junior sat down, slowly turning to face his monster whenever the thing took a turn around the room.

"I never thought I'd see him so crazy," Buddy said, as Mr. Pool came to sit again beside him. "Junior always was strange but I was used to it." All at once Buddy had cupped his hands close to his face, like he was going to sneeze. But he was sobbing, his shoulders heaving and shaking.

Mr. Pool held onto Buddy's arms. The boy's crying ended as abruptly as it had begun.

"It's a sad time," Mr. Pool told him, patting him, "a sad, sad time."

Then Buddy was talking. At last he was telling Mr. Pool all he could about who he was. "You see," Buddy was saying, "it's not just these planets here that we made, that you have now in the box. You see, there are planets all over this city. I am Tomorrow Billy. Tomorrow Billy! There are Billys all over this town!"

Buddy talked on. He told Mr. Pool about the beginning and the first Tomorrow Billy he had known when he was still a child. He told Mr. Pool about today, about his planet in the broken-down basement of a worn-out tenement house. He told of Nightman and of Franklin. He said to Mr. Pool all he had held back for as long as he could remember.

Through Buddy's confused and disconnected sentences, Mr. Pool pieced together the boy's story. By the time Buddy finished, Mr. Pool was sitting with his mouth open, his eyes bright with excitement. He understood what Buddy had been telling him but he couldn't quite let himself believe.

"Can it be true?" Mr. Pool said, searching Buddy's face. "Can something like this . . . really be true?"

"You come with me and you'll see whether I'm lying," Buddy told him.

"Oh, I don't mean to say you lie," Mr. Pool said. "I mean, I know you wouldn't lie. It's just that I never dreamed . . ."

". . . You come with me," Buddy said again. "We can take Junior. He can come live on my planet. Nobody'd ever find him."

"He'd freeze to death," Mr. Pool said absently, still searching Buddy's face.

"The point is," Buddy said, "I can do it, I can take care of him but I need your help. I can't do it by myself. I need supplies, someone on the outside. Not to feed us or anything, but just to be there in case of emergency. We've never had no one in case one of us is sick or hurt bad."

". . . have all the help you want," Mr. Pool said. He still couldn't quite grasp what Buddy had told him. Buddy could see that in Mr. Pool's eyes.

"You come with me," Buddy told him. "The only thing is, I don't know how I'll ever get Junior down my ladder, let alone that monster he sees . . ."

Mr. Pool smiled suddenly. The image of the thing Junior had with him, that unseen relative, going down a rope ladder was suddenly absurdly and diabolically funny. It brought Mr. Pool to his senses. Everything Buddy had told him came together in that one picture of a thing unseen going down in darkness to a place unknown.

"I have all kind of gear equipment in my car," Mr. Pool said, "I can fix up a hoist and winch in no time."

"Strong enough to carry Junior?" Buddy asked him.

"Strong enough to lift most any busted thing," Mr. Pool said. Then, pausing, "How much do you suppose a monster weighs?"

Buddy threw back his head and laughed. "Very . . . heavily . . ." he managed to say, and he laughed and laughed.

Mr. Pool held onto Buddy until Buddy had some control over his hysterical laughing.

"Didn't think I was going to stop," Buddy said finally.

"Too much has happened to you, and too fast," Mr. Pool told him. "Look, I'll get this box in my car; then I'll come back and we'll all go to . . . what do you call it again?"

"My planet," Buddy told him, "the planet of Tomorrow Billy."

The pride Mr. Pool felt looking at Buddy was more than he could ever say. He smiled warmly and then went about his work. Gently he placed the last planet, the planet of Junior Brown, in the carton with the rest of the solar system. The great brown planet was eclipsed, boxed in, gone as though it had never been. Mr. Pool turned the carton on its end and taped it closed. He heaved it up on his shoulder and carried it, coffinlike, out of the room.

When Mr. Pool returned, he and Buddy carried cartons of food out to the car, squeezing them in the truck with the maintenance equipment. They took the unopened containers of Chinese food which they could reheat later on. They took Junior's suitcase. Standing on the sidewalk, Junior waited for them to finish. The night was black and bitter cold but clear. City sounds echoed hugely.

Mr. Pool and Buddy eased Junior into the back seat of the car. The thing with Junior went in first, for Junior stood aside a moment to let him by. For an instant Buddy thought he felt something brush past him. He quickly got hold of himself.

"Don't you start," he told himself. "It ain't nothing but the cold air playing tricks."

Buddy got in the car in the front next to Mr. Pool. The five-foot carton was between them on top of the front seat and extending clear to the rear windows between Junior and the relative with him.

They were safe, once in the car. They all felt the comfort of this new hiding place. Mr. Pool turned on the ignition and the heater. Cold air blew around Buddy's legs but soon the air warmed. Mr. Pool turned on the head-lights. They eased out into traffic flowing down Broadway.

"Now this is cool," Mr. Pool told them. "I like having some traveling companions."

Buddy grunted. He was not used to auto-mobiles. He couldn't distinguish lights flash-ing through the windows.

"Never thought I'd be traveling down this street with a whole solar system and a monster besides," Buddy said.

"This life holds wonders for us all," Mr. Pool said and then, "how you doing back there, Junior?"

Junior was engrossed in the window lighting on and off, in shading the glass with the moisture of his breath.

"Do you suppose the relative is sitting there just like us, with his legs crossed and his hands folded?" Buddy said.

"How do you know he's got any hands to fold?" Mr. Pool said.

"Junior did say he is this dirty, crusted man."

"I wonder if he smells very bad," Mr. Pool said.

"Junior says he's pretty stinking but I can't smell a thing," Buddy said. Laughter welled up inside him. Buddy gave himself over to it for a moment, shaking soundlessly.

"Easy," Mr. Pool said, so softly Buddy barely heard him.

"It's not funny, is it?" Buddy said.

"No," Mr. Pool told him.

They fell silent. In no time they were close to where Buddy wanted to take them. Buddy told Mr. Pool about what they would have to do. They would have to work as quickly as possible in between the two buildings and right by the window where it was always dark.

For Junior, riding in the car with Buddy and Mr. Pool was contentment and as much as he could know and remember at one time. He'd already forgotten whatever it was Miss Peebs' relative had been telling him all this time. That

was because the relative never did stop talking
for long. Junior didn't much like him or what
he had to say. Sometimes Junior forgot the
relative was sitting next to him. Then light
would come bursting in Junior's head. Junior
would see that relative jumping around, getting the car dirty, and he would hear the relative as though his voice were coming through
a megaphone.

"GIMME SOME SKIN. SOME SKIN,
JUNIOR BLUEBLAM. MY MAN, MY
MAIN MAN."

"Shut off," Junior told him. The relative
looked mean. He was going to jump out of the
car and run away to Miss Peebs. So Junior
smiled at him. The relative liked to have
friends most of all. He stayed with Junior.

They reached the street where Buddy had
his planet. Mr. Pool took the car around the
block so they could come up to the building
and park on the same side. He and Buddy
unloaded everything in the passageway between the two buildings while Junior waited in
the car until they were ready for him.

"If I'm going to fix up a hoist, I'm going to
have to use my flashlight," Mr. Pool told
Buddy.

"How come you can't do it in the dark?"
Buddy asked him. They were talking as softly
as they could; their voices were indistinguish-

able from sounds of the city. But far below in Buddy's building, their voices had been heard.

"Because I got to make a differential which will give us the right amount of lifting power," Mr. Pool said to Buddy. "You can put yourself between my light and the street. Hand me those two sheaves."

Mr. Pool pointed the light so that Buddy could see in the gear box.

"Which are sheaves?" Buddy said.

"The grooved wheels," Mr. Pool told him. "One is bigger and one is smaller. They are wheels with a rim to guide the rope."

Buddy found the wheels. "Why is one bigger?" he wanted to know.

"That's the differential," Mr. Pool told him, his hands working expertly with rope and sheaves. "The diameter of one wheel is greater than the other. You add on this crank with a handle to transmit motion to the larger wheel. Some of the motion of the larger wheel is again transferred to the smaller wheel, which turns faster and adds more lift."

"I can't see it," Buddy said.

"You'll be able to see it, the motion," Mr. Pool said. "You just may not be able to understand the mechanics of it—how far do we have to bring Junior down?" he added.

"About eighteen, twenty feet," Buddy said.

Mr. Pool was silent. His hands moved with

precision and speed, winding heavy rope around the wheels. He tried not to think. He had no idea what he would find once he set up his hoist at the window. What was down there? Could Buddy be as out of his head as Junior? No. No, the boy had to be telling him the truth. But a planet of homeless children? Mr. Pool tried to keep his mind on his hands.

In fifteen minutes the hoist was ready. "We'll hook it over the windowsill," Mr. Pool told Buddy. "You'll have to watch that hook. You might even try pressing down on it all the time I'm lowering Junior. If you see that sill about to give up a splinter, you yell out. Now. Go get Junior."

"All right," Buddy said, "but first, the window."

Mr. Pool followed Buddy to the window. He had by this time turned off the flashlight. But Buddy didn't need light. From long practice he found the loose boards in the dark on his first attempt. He uncrossed the boards and leaned them against the building. Next Buddy pulled out in one piece the planks covering the window opening. Then he leaned through the opening as far as he could go without falling, bracing one hand on that foot-wide section of flooring left after the floor had caved in on the basement. He came back out of the window and turned to Mr. Pool.

"There's this little space of floor we've got to

knock away if that hoist is going straight down."

"It's got to go straight down," Mr. Pool told him.

Buddy leaned back into the window opening. It was black and still below in the basement. He leaned as far in as he could and yelled down, not loud, but with his voice as clear as he could make it. "Tomorrow Billy," he called. "Stay back, we got to knock out some floor."

No sound came from below. Buddy thought about the silence. No, they would be there— Franklin and Nightman and whoever else had come up from the bridge. They were just being smart, just staying loose and waiting.

Mr. Pool took up his hatchet and chopped away the floor in front of the windowsill and on each side of the sill as far as he could reach. "That ought to do it," he said when he had finished.

"Wait," Buddy said, "stay here." Buddy squeezed in beside Mr. Pool. "I just had this awful thought," he said.

"What's that?"

"I thought maybe Junior's too big to fit in this opening; but if both of us can, he can too."

"It might be tight, but he'll fit," Mr. Pool said.

Again Buddy peered down into the total darkness below them. "Tomorrow Billy," he called once more. "Give us some light." A long moment passed with no movement, nor any sound from the basement.

Mr. Pool felt his own heart seem to slow.

"Tomorrow Billy," Buddy called. "Nightman Black, Franklin—all my brothers—give me some light."

Nothing moved down in darkness that Mr. Pool could hear. He thought, Don't let him tell me they've gone. Don't let him do that.

Buddy had heard the smallest sound. He knew all of them were down there but he needed that sound to prove it to Mr. Pool when he knew Mr. Pool hadn't even heard. Yet, Buddy felt himself seem to calm. He had to smile. He waited.

The first glow came from the table against the basement wall, a soft puff of yellow light just strong enough to shadow a clump of dark figures.

Mr. Pool's breathing seemed to stop as the next glow came from close to the center of the room. The candle-glow moved in a tight arc as some boy set the patio candle down beside him. The third light came from the far wall dead center of the first and second glow.

Buddy figured there were at least eight boys down there, counting Franklin and Nightman. "Going to have a full house," he said softly, casually to Mr. Pool. "I'll go get Junior." He squeezed out of the window, leaving Mr. Pool staring.

Mr. Pool didn't move from the opening in the short time Buddy was gone. He continued to look down on the scene below. He knew that all of them down there were looking up at him, even though he couldn't see their eyes or any of their features. Mr. Pool simply felt their staring. Knowing he was there, they had no idea who he was. And having no idea about him, they made no move of any kind. That, Mr. Pool had time to think, was discipline.

"I got him," Buddy said, coming back to the window. "He was sitting there just how we left him and he's got the relative with him too."

Mr. Pool scooted out of the window opening. He shone his flashlight on the tool box and the hoist equipment on the ground. Placing the light next to the window, he attached a leather sling to the steel hook below the smaller wheel of the hoist. Next he fixed the top hook above the larger wheel to the window frame so that the smaller wheel and sling were below the window frame on the inside.

"Now," Mr. Pool said, "once Junior is sitting on the sill, we're going to shine the light down in there so he can get in the sling seat."

"Okay now, Junior," Buddy said, his voice soft, like a purr, "you come on over here."

Junior stood a great hulk of darkness against the building opposite Mr. Pool and Buddy. He didn't move.

"I'll bring him over," Mr. Pool said.

"No," Buddy told him. "He's waiting for me to do it." Buddy went over and took Junior by the arm.

Buddy felt Junior tense his body. "Okay, brother," Buddy said, "I'm going to lead you over to that window. All right. Take it easy now. Easy, Junior."

Buddy had Junior's arm and was steering Junior to the window. "Now, kneel down," Buddy told him. "You got to get in that opening and sit there and then you got to ease down into a sling Mr. Pool fixed up just for you. You can't see the sling from here because it's inside and below us in the dark. But we'll shine the flashlight down and you'll be able to see."

Obediently Junior allowed Mr. Pool and Buddy to lift him into the opening where the window had been.

"Shine the flashlight down from over his head," Mr. Pool told Buddy, "I'll keep hold on him as he slides down into the sling."

Buddy shone the light clear down on the sling and down to the basement floor. When Junior saw the distance below him, he hurled back in terror, knocking Buddy out of the way and falling out of the window onto the ground.

"Awh, Junior," Buddy said. "It's nothing. That sling is going to hold you. Mr. Pool fixed it himself."

"How far is home?" Junior said, these words the first he had spoken to them in all this time.

Mr. Pool and Buddy lifted Junior to a sitting position. They brushed off his raincoat as best they could. "Junior," Mr. Pool said, "do you want me to take you home?"

"He knows he can't go home. He don't mean it like that," Buddy said. "Listen," he said to Junior, "home is never far. You can always think about how close it is whenever you get homesick. It's just up and over town. Your maw hasn't gone no place. She's all right, you know that, because she's got the medicine and the oxygen. She knows you're O.K., too. But it never was your job to do, Junior. See, because it has to be your daddy's job to take care of her. Should have been, a long time ago to start. And your daddy's going to be home tomorrow. Your maw will be all right. You won't be far from her, Junior. Home is never far."

"I want him to go first," Junior said. He looked around behind him to the opposite wall where he had been standing.

It was Buddy who realized Junior meant for the relative to get into the sling and go down into the basement before he did.

"All right," Buddy said. He and Mr. Pool pulled slightly away from Junior.

"How do you call a monster?" Mr. Pool asked Buddy.

"You don't," Buddy thought to say. "You wait and you feel when it's time."

"You are better tuned than I am," Mr. Pool said. "You tell me when it's time."

Junior had to watch the relative act the fool in front of the window. The relative was pulling up his filthy socks and knocking the heels of his runover shoes into the ground like he was preparing to climb a mountain. "Fool. Stop it," Junior told him. "Get on in there. Get in before I send you home."

The relative backed off from Junior. Scared he would be left all by himself, he was able to climb into the window and into the sling. Once in the sling, he waited for the ride to begin.

"Time," Buddy said, after a moment. He focused the light on the empty sling as Mr. Pool turned the crank which began the process of lowering the sling to the basement floor.

When Mr. Pool had brought the sling up again, Buddy flashed the light on Junior.

"Time," he said to Junior.

Junior made the windowsill and holding himself tight as he could, he lowered himself into the sling with the help of Buddy and Mr. Pool.

"Just hold on to either side at the top," Mr. Pool told Junior. "Sit as still as you can. You may bump the wall once or twice but it ain't going to hurt."

Halfway down Junior saw all those figures in the soft glow of candlelight.

"More relatives?" he said to the thing waiting for him.

"*You brothers is lookin' forty mile, too,*" the thing told him.

"Didn't know I had some brothers," Junior said back to him. "Go on and sit down, fool." The relative strutted to the nearest wall. He sat himself neatly down, like he wasn't sick or anything.

Watching, Nightman and Franklin sat close together in the glow of the patio light on the table. For half an hour they'd listened and strained through the dark trying to hear what Tomorrow Billy was doing. Now they watched, fascinated, as this unbelievable fat boy came riding down on this sling, talking to himself a mile a minute.

"He got to weigh three hundred pound," Franklin whispered, as Junior, still talking, heaved himself out of the sling.

Nightman said nothing. He watched the huge fat boy hurl himself away from the mountain of debris on one side and the table on the other, over to the wall near where some new boys were sitting. The new boys moved just their heads to look at Junior. They saw how well Junior was dressed. They saw he was talking to someone unseen by them. Still, loose and ready, they kept their eyes on him.

Nightman and Franklin turned from the fat boy to see what else would happen up above them. They both wore green shawls, crocheted and delicately braided at neck and wrist. The shawls were warmer than they looked; Nightman's had no opening down the front. It pulled on over his head like a long nightshirt. He had used most of the spool of green string he had found on himself and Franklin. And he had bought four balls of twine to make heavy pullovers. Or, if he could, he would combine the balls of twine to make Tomorrow Billy the prettiest coat anybody ever did see.

From the window opening above came that sling carrying an old guy whose head was completely bald. The old guy looked straight at Nightman, grinning from ear to ear. He held onto the sling with one hand while clutching this great, long box tightly on his lap with the other.

It's all true, thought Mr. Pool. The planet of Tomorrow Billy. To think I could have missed it!

None of them, not even Franklin, said anything as the old guy carried the long carton to a space just outside the circle of light. Gently he set the box down and carefully positioned himself beside it.

"Nightman," Tomorrow Billy called from above. When Nightman heard his name, he moved out of the circle toward the window.

"Here comes a box of tools," Buddy told him. "Stay out of its way."

Nightman could see the box attached to the hook from which the sling had been suspended.

"Take the hook out when the box is on the ground," Buddy told him. Nightman did as he was told and then stood silently as the hook rose again. In a few minutes the hook came down with sacks of food attached. Nightman unhooked them and carried them to the table. Next came a suitcase. When Nightman had taken it over to the file cabinet, he came back to wait for his Billy. He watched as the Billy fitted the planks over the window opening, then stretched his legs out from the sill to grab the rope ladder between his ankles.

Buddy swung down his rope ladder. He came off the ladder breathing hard. Nightman stood before him, waiting.

Buddy had to smile. "I see you found what to do with that spool of string," he said.

"Yes, sir," Nightman said. He smoothed his hand over the shawl's intricate design he had woven with just his fingers.

Franklin came silently and stood next to Nightman.

"That's about the nicest-looking old string I ever seen," Tomorrow Billy told them.

"I tried to make 'em just alike," Nightman

said, "but I'd get to thinking about something and my hands would just go on and make something different."

"Don't ever try to make them just alike," Buddy said. "Just alike, you got yourself some uniforms and don't ever start making no uniforms."

"Yes, sir, I won't," Nightman said.

"I see we got us a full house," Buddy said. "You boys will have to help me. When did they get here?" He nodded toward the new boys up from the bridge.

"Just about right after dark," Franklin said. "They brought their own food with them and their own sleeping bags."

"Good," Buddy said. "Anything else?"

"Nothing," Franklin said. He looked at Nightman.

Nightman thought a minute. "Just that me and Franklin got along fine," he said. "We didn't do nothing wrong. I learn a lot. I got this job sweeping in a meat rendering plant where they make the soap."

"He already made ten dollar this week," Franklin said.

"We put it into some more food and a little pillow for me." Shyly Nightman grinned. "I like a pillow but I never did have one until now."

"You did fine," Buddy told them. "Now."

He looked up and around. The boys knew he had dismissed them and they went back to their seats next to the table.

Silence surrounded Tomorrow Billy as they all waited for him. He came closer to them, stopping at the edge of the light next to the box with the solar system, and Mr. Pool. For a long moment he stared at Junior Brown against the near wall. Junior grinned back at him. He seemed almost peaceful and he was no longer talking.

Buddy swayed on his feet. Mr. Pool and all the others saw in the forward slump of his shoulders how exhausted he was. But still he stood there, his mind a whir of thoughts as light as feathers floating on air.

It seemed to Buddy that he had in the room all he needed. There was Junior and Mr. Pool, there was Nightman, Franklin and the other boys, all together, all needing one another and him. He had the solar system. Maybe Mr. Pool would find a way to make it work. Maybe one day Doum Malach could come down and see what they had, see what Buddy had done for himself. Doum would see that he, Buddy, was Tomorrow Billy because he was the strongest and knew best how to survive.

Something nudged at Buddy deep within his mind. He recalled his first and only Tomorrow Billy and what the Billy had told those of his planet, that they must learn to live for themselves.

"No," Buddy said. They all heard him but they listened and waited.

"We'll all get to know one another," Tomorrow Billy said at last. "This here is Mr. Pool. He's got a surprise there in his box and he is going to help us along from the outside. Over there is Junior. We got to be nice to Junior and maybe we can fix up some old piano we might find for him. When it's safe, we can have him play for us. Junior can play the piano like nobody. Everybody is to see that Junior doesn't hurt himself.

"Over there is Nightman and Franklin," the Billy continued. "They been traveling together because Nightman was new with me only a few days ago."

Junior studied Buddy's face glowing with soft light. He laughed to himself, for his mind showed him Buddy swinging wild and cool through city streets. Buddy was waiting outside his house for him. He and Buddy took their time going down to the river. Junior was suddenly happy to remember.

"*Shoot*," the relative told Junior, "*don't you tell that lie. It never was like that*."

"Never?" Junior said.

"*You just made it up*," the thing said.

"Like I made you up?" Junior said. The relative said nothing. He became less clear to

Junior and somewhat fuzzy around his shoulders. The thing seemed to disappear part way into the wall. Junior rested, letting himself recognize the closeness of all of them together. The sound of Buddy's voice fell in a pattern of musical notations.

"We are together," Buddy told them, "because we have to learn to live for each other."

So that was it, he told himself. That was what he had forgotten all these years, or changed with the passage of time to fit with his loneliness. No, his Tomorrow Billy had taught him much more than life as mere survival.

"If you stay here, you each have a voice in what you will do here. But the highest law for us is to live for one another. I can teach you how to do that."

Buddy looked down at Mr. Pool. Their eyes held in a gaze affirming their faith in one another.

Buddy glanced over at Junior. Seeming to sleep, slumped down in the collar of his raincoat, Junior heard Buddy's words in music.

"I'll help you just as long as you need me to. I am Tomorrow Billy . . ." His instinct told him what to do as it always did. Buddy's face glowed with new light. ". . . and . . . this is the planet of Junior Brown."